MW00478731

Everybody Knows

Mike Wilson

ACKNOWLEDGEMENTS

This was not an easy process for me. In fact, I finished it several years ago and it has been sitting around collecting dust. I finally decided to move forward with self-publishing after learning to trust that my inner-circle would not steer me wrong.

First, I must thank Louise Ketz. She has dedicated her life to publishing and I met her after she'd retired. I work in a pub, and one afternoon she heard me talking to a friend about a writing idea I was working on. When she had a moment to talk to me in private, she was annoyed that I had not tapped her as a resource, and demanded that she see what I'd written. I told her that it wasn't finished but she insisted, so I reluctantly gave in. She read it within a few days, and became excited to see the finished product. It took me several months to finish, and I likely wouldn't have, had she not hounded me constantly. We then submitted to a few publishers that she was still in contact with, but were denied not because of the content, but because they were in need of longer novels to publish. This is that short novel.

My second THANK YOU goes to Theresa Caulfield. She is an avid reader and has read every word I've written since I started this adventure. She has constantly encouraged me to push on, write more and find a way to publish. I love you T!

Finally, a big THANK YOU goes to Matt Timney, Sarah Turco, Katy Coyle, Julie Behuniak, Fernando Marulanda, Robert Carroll, and Adrian Cooper. All have read this manuscript, and all have pushed me to keep at it.

Every one of these people has been extremely kind and encouraging to me. They have believed in me, and that is often more than I can say for myself.

~ Mike Wilson

Everybody Knows

Annie—
Thanks for all the years
of laughter and support!
Go Mets!

CHAPTER ONE

Pedro opened his eyes and looked at his alarm clock. It was 4:11 a.m. In four minutes the most annoying sound of the day would tear through the morning quiet. He looked at the ceiling and wondered in the silence why he woke up early this morning. The fresh air from the cracked window across the room washed over his face and he decided that it was time to get the day started. He rolled over, clicked off the alarm switch, and swung his legs down to the floor where his house slippers waited to shuffle around the apartment and start another day.

He had a weird knot in his stomach, a ping of worry that occurred from time to time when things weren't quite right. His daughter was in kindergarten and often his worries were directly connected to her. It was late September and school had been going well for her thus far, so that didn't seem to be it. He turned and looked at the long black hair of his wife that always seemed to shine, even in the dark. After a yawn and a stretch, he grabbed his robe from the hook on the wall and headed for the bathroom.

The shower was hot this morning, a pleasant surprise that seemed to happen only a few times a week. As the water kept constant pressure on his back, the nerves in his stomach seemed to hold the attention of his thoughts. Rinsing the shampoo out of his short hair and turning around a few times to get the soap off of his body seemed to go slower than usual, and the excitement of a hot shower didn't seem to matter this morning. He turned off the water, dried off, brushed his teeth and put his robe back on before scooting into the kitchen.

~

Pedro was a Mexican immigrant who had been in the United States for twelve years. He had received his papers to make him a legal citizen the previous year, but it was a process that seemed to take forever. He hopped the border when he was 23 years old and after a very hot and long journey, finally arrived in New York City. He had several cousins and a brother already living and working there. He bounced from sofa to sofa when he arrived until he was able to find some work and eventually get a tiny apartment in Queens. His rent was paid in cash every month and he was usually a week early with payment. He was determined not to draw any attention to himself or get in any sort of misunderstanding that could get him sent back to Mexico.

Through a recommendation from his brother, Pedro landed a job as a porter at a small pub in Manhattan. He had to be there 6 days a week and had to have the entire bar cleaned and set up by 10:30 a.m. every day. He had replaced another Mexican porter whose father took ill, requiring a return to Mexico to be with him. The pay was 40 bucks a day plus a few extra bucks the bartender usually left for him. Since he was done and out the door by 11:00 every morning, he was able to have another job for the rest of the day. He sent half of his income home every month to help with his rather large family still residing in Mexico City.

Reina and Pedro met two years after he arrived in New York. She was also 25 at the time and was working as a teller at a bank when Pedro came in to make a deposit. From that moment on, he made sure he made the deposit on the same day at the exact same time every week to share the few cordial words required between customer and teller. He admired her fluency with English and the ease with which she seemed to interact with her customers and co-workers. He made sure he complimented her every time he saw her, be it her perfume, earrings, hairstyle, manicure or choice in costume jewelry decorating her fingers. As the weekly visits went by, the conversation loosened up and the jokes came naturally. The day she said "Hola Pedro" before he even stepped to the counter became the favorite day of his life.

Reina accepted an offer to join Pedro and his cousins in their weekly soccer game on a Sunday afternoon. The men played for an hour or two on the edge of a park where grass struggled to survive. After the game, everyone retreated to the apartment of the rotating host for some food and drinks. That was the day she became a member of the family. They married just a year later in a small ceremony in Queens, NY, with both families attending.

Reina being born in the U.S. was a huge benefit to Pedro once they were married. The paperwork for citizenship was much less complicated and the benefits of Reina working full time at a large bank took care of insurance and tax issues. He was never really comfortable accepting these benefits but there was nothing shady about it, he loved Reina, she loved him, and marriage was just the next step. The politics of the situation was not his fault.

~

Breakfast was always a glass of orange juice and an apple picked up from the fresh fruit stand on the way home the evening before. He liked to cut his apple with a small knife and eat it in slices. There's just something manly about eating it that way. It was always about 10 minutes, enough time to check out the weather and make sure there were no subway problems on the news. This morning was no different and the commute looked to be a breeze so he moved quietly into his room to get dressed without waking his wife. He always kissed her cheek on the way out, to which she always stirred a bit, but never really woke up. She'd promised time and again that this didn't disturb her slumber so he always kissed her goodbye.

Their daughter didn't really have her own room. She slept in a twin bed across the large room behind an old wardrobe partition. She had a tiny nightstand with a light next to her bed so she felt like she had her own room. Pedro actually preferred that for now, he couldn't stand the thought of an actual wall separating his daughter from him. He snuck around the corner, gave her a peck on the forehead, and headed for the door.

~

The subway is never crowded at 4:45 a.m. Coming from Queens, the folks are usually doing the same thing Pedro is doing, heading to some sort of service job in the city. He always tried to guess what each person was off to do. He could pick out the hotel-cleaning people the easiest. Construction guys were obvious. Chefs or cooks generally wore some sort of clog on their feet tattooing their profession. Many were Nanny's, some were maids, and others were porters, busboys, waiters, and food runners. When all else failed, he simply hoped that whatever their occupation called for, they were safe and happy in this big crazy city.

The ride into Manhattan was only about 20 minutes. The smell of hot coffee and breakfast sandwiches in the train cars was a nice contrast to the smell of garbage and urine one has to soak up just prior to getting in one. There was always enough room for a seat, which allowed him to read through the paper on the way to work. He scrolled the headlines, looked at the Yankee scores from the previous day, and read *page six* every day. That was his favorite part of the paper, the gossip section in the New York Post. It amazed him how carefree some people in the world actually were, and examples of that silly sense of freedom were splattered all over the Post every day, pictures included!

Folding his paper in half and tucking it under his arm as he rose up from his seat he again remembered the strange knot in his stomach. His wife and daughter were fine, he double-checked that he locked the door on his way out and he had his keys for both home and the pub. As he walked out of the subway exit, he decided that he would call home this afternoon and talk to his mother. It had been two weeks. Maybe that was it. Yeah, that had to be it. Everything else was fine.

~

The late summer air in Manhattan can have a million different textures from day to day and sometimes from block to block. Pedro loved it on the occasions when the scent of the ocean had settled over the streets of the city. He would close his eyes, stand still and breathe deep for a moment imagining he was on the water. On the best days, he could get all the way to work inhaling the ocean. More often than not however, it would be interrupted by the stench of garbage from a restaurant, the vomit of a drinker who had a few too many, or the exhaust of a vehicle sitting at a stoplight. The sidewalks were just starting to be sprayed down and rinsed off by porters and building workers. Brooms sweeping the concrete and bread and newspapers being delivered all around made this a very typical stroll to work.

Pedro always walked the same route from the train to the pub. There was no reason really; it was 5 blocks from the train stop and any combination of routes was the same distance. It was just being a creature of habit that made this particular route the one he walked. He often saw all the same people on his route and head nods were common. The final turn of the five-block journey passed a little deli where he always grabbed a coffee and a daily number lotto ticket with his daughters' birthday being his lucky numbers. He played 50 cents midday and 50 cents evening. His total was $1.85 every morning, but today he bought a one-day pack of vitamins for an extra dollar because he figured maybe he was missing something in his diet that was making his stomach nerves knot up.

As he stepped out of the corner store and looked up the block toward the bar, he paused for a second. Something wasn't right. It was nothing really; a light by the door had not been shut off, but unusual for sure. Even on nights when the bartenders stayed late and had a drink or a smoke, that light was turned off. It was flipped off when last call was given to the customers to try to deter latecomers on the streets from coming in and begging for one final concoction.

Furthermore, it was Tuesday morning. Monday night was Cliff's shift.

"Que raro." Pedro thought.

As he started to walk again, his stomach was tighter than it had been all morning. He almost felt like he could be sick. He picked up his pace a bit just in case that was the situation. He would much rather be inside the pub and able to puke in a trash bin or the toilet instead of on the street where people were definitely beginning to stir. A jogger passed him as he reached for his keys and approached the front door. He set his coffee down on the step in front of the door and he could see a TV was still on through the window. "There is definitely something wrong," he thought and he confirmed it when he put his key in the lock. It simply turned with ease making Pedro's heart jump at the unlocked door. He picked up his coffee, put his key in his pocket, moved his paper to the other armpit, and pulled the door slowly. A strange smell erupted out of the cracked door. What he saw when he stepped in sent an instant stream of tears running down his cheeks.

CHAPTER TWO

Cliff Barry was 27 years old, dusty blond hair, square jaw and broad shoulders. His days were spent at the gym or in the park and his nights were full of drinks and dates. If he wasn't working, he was at another bar making friends, flirting with pretty ladies and trying to find the next hot tip in the stock market. He was very friendly and well liked. He had a knack for spotting trouble in advance and usually left the scene before things got out of hand. On occasion, he'd hang back if he felt he was needed because his fellow bar crew was understaffed. Most of the time, he just enjoyed the company of people celebrating the moment. He was a good fit for the bar scene in Manhattan, both behind it and in front of it.

Lucky as he was to be debt free at his age, Cliff was far from cheap. On his nights out, he would easily blow through fifty bucks and often twice that. On the other hand, he was very diligent with a budget. Most people on a set income had their bills figured out monthly, the life of a bartender was better taken a week at a time. It was simple really; the first $360.00 per week went into an envelope for rent (heat and water included), another envelope got the next $200.00 for the stock market, the third received $30.00 to cover the monthly expenses of his gym membership and two websites he had a paid subscription with, and the fourth got $65.00 for his cell phone, electric, internet and basic cable bills. To continue to stay debt free and stay above water while investing, he had to earn a minimum of $750.00 per week, with the "envelope system" getting $655.00. The remaining $95.00 was plenty to cover daily expenses and food. This budget worked well for him because he actually averaged an income of about $1,000.00 per week, which allowed him to have the social life he enjoyed. He started each week at zero, so anything left in his pocket at that time went into a savings account for vacationing, holiday travel and gifts. It was down to a science.

The stock market was something that intrigued Cliff since he was old enough to balance a checkbook. He never wanted to be a broker, never wanted a screaming boss and couldn't imagine spending 70 hours a week in a monkey suit behind a desk with a phone stuck to his ear. The idea of investing other people's money never interested him either. He much preferred his own investing, done online and worry free. The money was his to work with, money he'd earned, which made him accountable to nobody but himself. After 3 years of investing 10k per year, his portfolio had already become slightly over forty-five thousand dollars. Though he didn't share his finances with anybody, he was privately very proud of the gains he'd accomplished. He dreamed of having 100k in the market by the time he was 30 years old so he could then move on to other investment ventures.

Often times Cliff would listen at a distance to investment type guys while working behind the bar. He'd jot down notes on a scratch of paper and do the research the following day. He was constantly reading investment magazines and books. Warren Buffet was his hero. He was a patient investor, not looking for an immediate turnaround on any one stock because he had a job and his bills were paid. He did triple up on a pharmaceutical company once, which gave him some leverage to put into some of the blue chips and start getting solid dividends. He was content with his self-educated foundation and loved to talk about the stocks with the Wall Street types he'd gotten to know. They never really knew how much of their information he was soaking up.

~

Montana was the perfect place to grow up in the 80's and 90's. Cliff grew up in the western part of the state in a town called Missoula. It was a gorgeous little town with mountains on all sides. The skiing and snowboarding were wonderful but the winters were long, though relatively mild. He grew up with his younger brother, Calvin, living in a small house with their mother. Cliff's folks divorced when he was seven years of age and Calvin was four. She worked at a local hospital as a nurse. Their father lived only a few miles away and was the head groundskeeper for the University of Montana, also in Missoula. Neither remarried and both were very active in raising their boys.

The two brothers knew most of the town growing up. They played baseball, football, and basketball throughout their childhoods. They spent the winter weekends on the slopes or hunting with their father and hiking and fishing in the summers. They were typical Montana boys, strong and tough with big hearts.

Both went to the University of Montana primarily because of finances. Living at home saved plenty of money and they got an education at a discount since their father was an employee. Neither was an honor student and both graduated with just a generic business degree, but at least it was a degree. Their mother wouldn't see it any other way. They earned money working at the Snowbowl Ski Lodge whenever possible. It was a scenic 30-minute drive from home until Cliff eventually became a bartender just off campus in the evenings during his senior year of school.

After college, Calvin opted to stay in Missoula and continue working the winters at ski lodges and owned his own mowing and landscaping company in the summer. He married a gorgeous little blond named Sally that he met at the university. She was in school for nursing when they met and eventually got a job at the same hospital as the boys' mother. Cliff wanted to try something else so after saving money for a year post college, many pleas not to go from his family, he packed a truck and headed east to New York City.

~

Cliff called home almost every day and spoke to somebody in the family. He basically rotated between mother, father and grandparents. He talked to Calvin almost every day. He missed his family a great deal and was extremely thankful for the technology today allowing him so many avenues of contact. If he couldn't get somebody on the phone, an email or a text message always sent some sort affection back west. That level of care and loyalty was embedded in him, and it was quickly the magnet for the hundreds of friends he now had in New York.

There is a strange loneliness that is found in major metropolitan communities. It is easy to think that with close to ten million people living in such a relatively close space, one would never be alone. Cliff was surprised to find that this was not the case. After only a few short months of living here, he understood why the rest of the country thought that New York was a cold and rude place. It was much like being the new kid in a new town joining a new high school. The cliques were already there. Everybody has their social circles and groups of friends and just like high school; they are not quick to welcome the newcomers.

Lucky for Cliff, his good looks and charm were very welcoming. Unfortunately, they welcomed all types of folks. He accepted invites for activities from many different people initially, but soon became much better at reading personalities. After landing a job at a pub called "The Tan Hat Man," his immediate social circle became those also working in the service industry. They were a handful of bartenders and servers that spent after hours at the Tan Hat Man. They gladly introduced him around the city to various people and great little hangouts full of friends that accepted him based on the recommendations of the company kept. With a little foundation settled, he was able to sift through the masses of people desperate for some sort of companionship and spend time with people that actually interested him.

~

It was a typical tiny Manhattan studio apartment a few blocks from the pub. An ad on Craigslist.com was where Cliff found the place, and after meeting the owner of the apartment and laying out three months rent in advance on the day he arrived in New York, it was now his home. The entire apartment was about the size of the family room of the house he grew up in. He wasn't there enough to need any more space. He slept and showered there and if it was nasty weather outside, it was a nice place to read or catch up on some television. The place was filled with his few belongings. A bed and a dresser lined one wall. A TV and the small computer desk fit nicely on the other. He had a big papasan chair awkwardly placed at the end of the room next to the window and was easily moved around, depending on visitors. His snowboard leaned against the corner in a travel bag and a mountain bike hung from the ceiling. Opposite the window was a tiny kitchen with the bathroom and a small closet down a very short and narrow hall. It was a nice little bachelor pad and it was cozy.

Cliff loved fresh air. The window was always open in the summer and cracked even during the coldest of winter nights. He preferred an oscillating fan to air-conditioning but always accommodated the comfort of his guests when he had them. The first thing he noticed whenever he visited home was the smell of real fresh air as he stepped off the plane in Montana. Fresh cut grass and the breeze off the mountains was extremely cleansing since living in a city with such a mixture of odors in the atmosphere. Not only was the air polluted with a variety of smells but also a variance of sounds. Sirens, horns and chatter among pedestrians took some getting used to.

The only person that had a key to Cliff's apartment beside himself was a tall, athletic, gorgeous young woman named Katy. She was an international flight attendant based out of John F. Kennedy Airport and often had afternoons off allowing for the two of them to explore the city together. She had relocated to the city from Nebraska and they had a lot in common. They spent many a day bouncing around the city and many nights she would stay with him.

She had two roommates so it was nice to be able get away from the girls she lived with and have a touch of space without gossiping about other girls, dates and relationships. She and Cliff weren't an official "couple" but it was pretty much accepted that it was only a "talk" away.

CHAPTER THREE

The smell of a pub is relatively distinct. The air is usually made up of a mix of grease from the grill and the unmistakable scent of beer. Depending where you are in the world, the aroma of cigarette smoke can add to the atmosphere that was home to the nightly festivities. Pedro did not expect to come to work and find those scents replaced by the odors of blood and sweat, like that of an athletic locker room, but with a strange essence of fear and rage stirred in. It hit him like a punch in the nose when the door swung open.

The view was even worse. There were stools thrown around, on their sides, upside down. Two tables were overturned, others shoved in all different directions. Glasses were broken on the bar and on the floor. There was not a single pool cue in the wall mounted rack. They were thrown all over the bar, some broken, most of them with blood drying and dripping all over the place. There was blood everywhere, splattered around the floor, the bar, the tables, the pool table. It was worse than anything Pedro had ever seen in a movie or imagined in his worse nightmare. The music was still on and it was loud.

After taking a moment to process that what he was witnessing was real, Pedro let the door close behind him and moved toward the opposite end of the bar where the phone was located. He stepped over stools and tried not to touch anything or step in blood. As he approached an overturned table, his heart stopped. Cliff's foot was motionless. Pedro moved quickly to see if Cliff was breathing. He hopped over another stool, grabbed the table by the top and slid it behind him. Cliff was lying on his stomach in a massive pool of blood. His face had been torn open at his cheek bone leaving a gaping gash where blood had pooled up. Pedro knew immediately that Cliff was dead. He knelt down to be sure, but saw that his right eye was open and clearly hadn't blinked in awhile. Pedro was sick, he turned and lumbered toward the waste basket and vomited all over the floor just before he reached it. Tears were screaming down his face, he couldn't get his breath and his knees were now buckled. This was not supposed to happen to Cliff. This was not supposed to happen at all.

He quickly gathered himself, stood up with all his strength, and grabbed the phone from the corner of the back bar, which was off the hook. He pushed the button to hang it up for a second before releasing it to hear a dial tone. He dialed the home number of the owner with his index finger even though it was shaking so much he had to concentrate to hit the correct numbers. After two rings the other end was connected with the owner sleepily saying "What's going on Pedro?"

~

The Tan Hat Man was a neighborhood staple on the Upper East Side of Manhattan for 13 years. It was owned and operated by a retired carpenter named Conrad. His wife had passed 6 years prior to his retirement so he took the money they'd saved to travel and bought a bar. Traveling was not something he wanted to do without her. He always enjoyed a nightlife so owning his own spot allowed for him to stay busy and enjoy a social life at the same time. He was 75 years old now and with only two years left on his current lease, he was going to allow it to expire and move into full retirement. He thought he may finally be able to do a little traveling as long as it involved fishing.

The pub didn't make much money. Conrad was much more interested in making sure his customers had a great time and his staff made plenty of money. Since the bar was bought with most of his life savings he only had to make sure that he made enough to replenish it, which he accomplished in just under five years. The business strategy he used was often frowned upon among other bar owners in the area but since Conrad was so well liked and respected, they never really gave him a hard time. When other bars were empty and trying to rustle up business, The Tan Hat Man had plenty of patrons. He ran specials both day and night, seven days a week. He believed in a little profit over a long time versus a lot of profit a few weeks a year. He allowed his crew to buy the regular customers a drink whenever they felt it necessary which created solid relationships and trust with his staff. Most of the people in his employ had been there for several years.

Conrad met Cliff the same week he had moved to the city. Without a job upon arrival and with only enough savings to last about six weeks, Cliff set out on foot and visited all the bars he could during the first week of his new life. The Tan Hat Man was the fifth place he visited and Conrad happened to be the first person he met when he walked in with his resume. After a short interview, Conrad explained that he had a guy leaving for law school the following week and had not replaced him yet. There were only three shifts available but they were shifts he wanted a male to work because there was no reason to pay for a doorman or security on Sunday, Monday and Tuesday nights. More shifts would become available for pickup depending on the time of year, but those three were steady. He generally hired people through recommendations or reputations but seemed to like Cliff right away. The next night Cliff came in to train and learn the ropes. The following week he was figuring out the trade of a Manhattan bartender which can really only be learned with the old sink-or-swim philosophy. Conrad spent the duration of every shift Cliff worked for a full month before allowing him to close up the place on his own. They became pals very quickly and The Tan Hat Man's customers seemed excited to give the new kid in the neighborhood a chance.

~

Conrad felt a jolt that rivaled that of an electric shock when he heard the fear in Pedro's voice mixed with the extremely loud music in the background. It took a moment for Pedro to find the words that explained he'd walked in on Cliff's lifeless body. Conrad immediately instructed Pedro not to move and call 911. He jumped out of bed, threw on his jeans, sneakers and a T-shirt and went racing out of his apartment with his cell phone open. He scrolled down to Detective Nelson and hit "talk" as he was practically sprinting the 6 blocks from his apartment building to get to his bar. Almost as soon as he'd hit the button he was connected to the voice that sounded all business answering, "Nelson."

"Nelson, its Conrad. My porter thinks my bartender is dead. Are you in the neighborhood?"

"Are you okay Conrad? You're wheezing"

"I'm fine! I'm running to my bar, are you around?"

"I can be. I'm a few blocks away. What's going on?" Nelson replied with a heightened sense of curiosity.

"I just told you my porter thinks my fucking bartender is dead! I'll see you there." Conrad snapped his phone closed and rounded the corner to the front of the bar.

He swung the door open and froze at the sight. Pedro was still on the phone in the corner with his finger in his other ear and visibly shaking as he was trying to give the emergency operator the information she was asking. The first set of lights seemed to nudge Conrad back to reality as he turned around to see Detective Nelson's police car arrive. He slowly stepped back out of the bar to address the detective but couldn't even raise his hand for a greeting. He just stood there blank and speechless as Nelson went immediately for the door.

~

Conrad had known Detective Nelson since he opened The Tan Hat Man. Nelson was only a police officer at the time and many of the guys on the force would stop in after their shifts for a drink and wind down for an hour or two. He made detective five years later and his co-workers celebrated the promotion with him at their favorite watering hole. It was a popular hangout and Conrad allowed them two-for-one drink specials anytime they stopped by.

Every social environment lends itself as a place for people to meet and create friendships and relationships. Conrad was such a social person that it was easy for people to warm up to him. He considered and expected his employees to be a reflection of himself. They would drink and watch games together, talk sports or even go golfing on their days off. Many genuine friendships were created in pubs all over the city and Conrad was always thankful to be a part of that.

Since the guys and girls "on the job" were such big fans of The Tan Hat Man, they would drive by several times a night and check in with Conrad and his staff. They would come to a slow roll in front of the bar and blink the spotlight one time at the window of the bar. This always got the attention of the bartender or bouncer and usually was returned with a quick salute signifying all was running smooth. On a rare occasion, a wave would call the officers to a halt. They would stop and be met by the bouncer, bartender or Conrad at the door to find out why they were beckoned. Those occasions were usually due to an unruly drunk or a fight close to breaking out which always seemed to diffuse as soon as the police appeared. Very few incidents occurred in Conrad's place. A good friendly staff, a very regular crowd, and a solid police presence were a good part of the fun and gentle presence of The Tan Hat Man.

~

Detective Nelson immediately got on his radio when he entered the bar. He quickly ordered any available cars to the scene as well as the Homicide Unit. He carefully maneuvered his way towards Pedro while he was hanging up the phone after confirming to the operator that the police had arrived. He told Pedro to hold still as he approached and leaned down to check Cliff's motionless, breathless body. After confirming Cliff was dead, Nelson looked and Pedro and quietly said, "Have you been in the basement yet?" Pedro slowly shook his head "no" as the front door was opening again with two more officers standing at the ready. "Come with me Pedro," Nelson again said just loud enough to be heard over the blaring sound system. "Stay right behind me and try not to touch anything."

When they reached the door one of the officers took Pedro aside to get any information he could provide. Nelson informed the other officers, now 5 strong, that though unlikely, the perpetrators could still be in the establishment somewhere. He instructed two of them to go to the fire exit on the side and stay there until the place had been thoroughly searched. He and the other officers then carefully walked the bar, flashlights and guns sweeping the scene. After checking both the men's and ladies restrooms, under and around the tables, pool table and behind the bar, they needed to secure the basement. Nelson reached behind the bar and pulled the plug on the stereo console to stop the music. The three of them took a moment to let their ears adjust and decide how to safely handle the narrow stairs and the basement. If the criminals were there, they would be cornered and have no way of escape. There was no need for unnecessary risk.

The steps were half the width of a normal set of stairs. They decided to go down one at a time, each taking a position until all three were safely down. It was dark and shadowy but within a few minutes and working in a three man rotation, they were positive that whoever had been here was now gone. The door to the office appeared to have been kicked several times based on the dents and dirty smudged shoe prints, but was still securely closed and locked.

Quickly moving back up the stairs, the two patrolmen headed to the front door and awaited instruction while detective Nelson stood next to Cliff's body and looked around. The fight that occurred here was brutal and intense. The beating Cliff endured was gruesome. Based on nothing more than observation, everything in the bar seemed to have been used at some point during the battle and Cliff must have held his own for some time because it didn't seem possible that all of the blood flung around was his. "I hope you got some good licks in buddy." Nelson mumbled to himself.

Two more detectives arrived at the front door announcing, "Homicide" as they took a short step inside. Nelson moved slowly toward them and stopped, turned back and moved swiftly toward the pool table. He remembered seeing something that didn't register when they first swept the bar looking for the suspects. He knelt next to the pool table with his flashlight and saw a cell phone on the floor that appeared to have blood not only on it, but *in* it. He stood, turned and barked, "Fellas, I need that phone! Take your pictures and get that open, I wanna know if it's still working and when that last call was placed!"

CHAPTER FOUR

Cliff woke up before his alarm clock buzzed on this, his last day on earth. There was a wonderful summer breeze coming through the window that seemed to kiss his face until he woke. It was a much more pleasant way to rise than when his eardrums were rattled by the sound of a clock with an attitude. Katy was lying next to him sound asleep so he quietly hit the stove to scramble some eggs, fry up some bacon and toast some whole wheat bread. If a fresh breeze wasn't enough to stir the sleeping beauty, a home cooked breakfast was sure to do the trick.

Once the bacon was popping and the bread was surrounded by orange coils, he stepped into the bathroom to wash his face and brush his teeth. When he returned to scramble the eggs, flip the bacon and butter the toast, Katy had expectedly sat up in bed. A smile and a yawn were shot across the room and Cliff grabbed a couple of plates and filled two glasses with orange juice. He dressed the plates, turned off the stove and headed her way for a cozy breakfast in bed. He kissed her on the cheek and said, "Good morning darlin'." She grinned and dove into her glass of orange juice.

After breakfast they turned on the television and watched some late morning programming before showering and heading outside for a little jog and a couple hours of sunshine in the park. Katy and Cliff were both into fitness so it was never even really a discussion. They both ran almost every day and often together. They were both members of the local runners club and competed in any races available on the weekends when she wasn't out of town for work. Today was a solid 4-mile run and then a leisurely stroll through Manhattan's Central Park before buying two bottles of water and finding a spot in some grass to sit and soak up the sun. They talked about work and schedules and tried to plan when they could see each other in the coming days. There wasn't a cloud in the sky.

Katy had to work in the early evening so they headed back to Cliff's place so she could gather her things and get on her way. She always gave him a big kiss before she left and today was not exception. It just seemed a little softer, a little nicer and a little more intimate. She left floating and Cliff took a moment to recognize he may really be falling for this girl. He wondered if she was feeling the same way.

~

Cliff jumped on the computer to check his portfolio and make sure there was no stock news he should be immediately aware of. He picked up his phone and dialed up his brother for their daily chat. On the nights he had to work, he always tried to catch

Calvin during a lunch break that never seemed to be taken at the same time. He was happy to hear that he caught him at the perfect time today. It was a typical brotherly talk; wife was fine, Mom and Dad were good, and football was starting up. Calvin had decided to be an assistant coach to a little league team this season, something Cliff wanted to do someday as well.

Just as he got off the phone with Calvin, his phone buzzed with an incoming text message. Tommy was a bartender at another pub a few blocks from The Tan Hat Man and wanted to see if Cliff wanted to grab a bite before they both had to be at work. A return text decided they would meet in an hour. Cliff jumped in the shower for the second time of the day and threw on his shorts and a T-shirt that bared the name of his job across the front.

As he walked out of his apartment his phone was buzzing again. He answered as he locked his door to find that another friend of his, Jeff, had knocked off work early and wanted to join for a bite and a beer. Two is company. Three's a crowd. They all met at a bright corner bar of Mexican influence and jumped into Margarita's and burritos while catching up on the week's sports. The day was perfect so far. Cliff was looking forward to a great night at work.

~

After two drinks and a healthy plate of food, the boys paid their tab and headed off to their evening destinations. Cliff stopped at the deli to grab a paper, a power bar and a Gatorade as he strolled to work. He chatted with a couple of other customers in the place that recognized him from the pub and after a short wait in line, he paid for his items with a twenty. His change included two fives. On a whim he told the clerk to give him two five-dollar scratch-off lotto tickets before he headed out the door en route to work.

He arrived at work about twenty minutes early. Handshakes and head nods were the usual greetings when Cliff arrived for his shift. He'd stop and chat with the folks finishing up happy hour as he slowly moved through the bar toward the stairs to the basement. Arriving at work often felt like he was the star quarterback showing up for the game. A kiss on a cheek to a lady or a handshake turned into fist knot completed with a shoulder-bump-hug and a pat on the back was common with the gents. It was a cool little ritual, one that he was sure he wouldn't get to participate in if he had a stuffy corporate job.

The office was a cramped little space in the corner of the basement with room for no more than two people. Cliff flopped in the desk chair and swiveled around to the safe to make his cash register for the evening. He spun the combination left and right in a flurry and pushed the handle down so the safe door would swing open. It was stuffed with important papers and documents, policies, earning reports, cash and coin. He pulled out what he needed to load up the till, counted it out quickly, and closed the door to the safe. A spin of the dial securely locked the tiny vault.

The shift started in five minutes so Cliff headed out of the office with his bank, closed and locked the door behind him and headed toward the stairs to the bustle of the building bar crowd. He exchanged hellos in Spanish to the delivery and kitchen folks on his way and was soon in the mix behind the bar. The daytime bartender was a feisty little bottle blond that everybody called Lexi, short for Alexandra. She gave him the scoop on the days happenings, explained the tabs she still had open, and pointed out a friend of hers visiting from out of town. After swapping the tills in and out of the register, she quickly moved toward the basement shouting thanks and goodnights to her crowd from the day. Cliff logged in to the computer, closed his drawer, and turned around to take his role in continuing the party.

~

For bars that stay open until 4:00 in the morning, the shift generally starts at 8:00 p.m. Not only does that make for a nicely packaged eight-hour shift, but it tends to be the time when the happy hour attendees head home for the evening creating a lull in business for an hour or so. Many happy hour folks use the change in bartenders as their cue to head home. The crowd replenishes with dates and night drinkers over the next couple hours to push the shift through the evening and into the morning.

Cliff always wondered what his last night behind a bar would be like. He pictured a big party with all of his friends and customers coming by to wish him luck as he moved on to bigger and better things. Since he had no idea what the bigger and better things were at this stage of his life, it never occurred to him that the farewell would be tonight. It was a nice surprise when the usual crowd didn't disperse immediately but seemed to hang around for one last drink. Everybody was in good spirits and as people did filter out, they seemed extra generous. They left an extra dollar or two in tips or made sure they had his attention to say goodnight. More hugs and kisses than usual were coming at him. For some reason, it didn't seem like anybody really wanted to leave. Many customers that he hadn't seen in weeks or months were popping in and it looked to be a very good night for his pocket.

The conversation amongst the surrounding crowd was the usual. The Jets and the Giants were sure to provide an exciting football season. The Mets and the Yankees were both on the bubble for making the playoffs. The topics always shifted as the hours passed. Who was the best pitcher ever? Who was the best running back of all time? Then on to what was on TV and what was on the radio these days, which in turn led to TV not being what it used to be and music today is not music etc... Before long it got into girls on guys and the reverse, which segued nicely to the best part of the evening: the sex talks. Everybody chimed in on why some guys do some things and why some girls won't do other things. It was a nightly ritual and Cliff thought he could probably predict what conversations were going to pop up within a half hour accurately. It was always fun.

It was usually midnight before Cliff could actually stand still for a moment and throw his thoughts in on the topic at hand. Dates were generally ending very good or ending very bad. Couples were tired and ready to go home and finish off the evening properly. The remaining folks were small groups of friends and co-workers and the regular patrons that showed up solo to mingle with the other regulars and chat with Cliff. The delivery guys were finishing up and cashing out, the kitchen staff cleaned up and headed home, and the waitress had closed out her last table and cleaned up her station. By 12:30 a.m., it was just Cliff and about twenty stragglers who clearly didn't have to be up at the crack of dawn.

~

It was about 1:00 a.m. when Cliff remembered that he had bought a couple lotto tickets. He pulled them out of his back pocket and the usual jokes about splitting it with everybody if he won were tossed about. They all had a good laugh as he began to scratch away. He handed the other ticket to a cute twenty-something at the end of the bar that was doing her best to get Cliff's attention. He said, "Here, if it's more than a hundred bucks, I'll take you to a nice dinner next week." Everybody laughed as she took a coin and scratched away. Cliff had finished his ticket and threw it at Pauly, who as stereotypes would have it, was the house bookie for the majority of the regulars that gambled. It was a loser and everybody got a good laugh. A minute or so passed and conversation was just getting started again when a squeal interrupted the group. Cliff looked at the young lady with a smile and laughed assuming she was trying to pull one over on him. She squealed again and somewhere in the middle said, "You won Cliff! You won!"

"No way." Cliff sarcastically replied

"Yes you did! You hit the jackpot! Five Hundred Thousand Dollars!"

Cliff snatched it out of her hand and looked over the ticket furiously figuring she had to have read something wrong. After a careful but quick examination, he said, "holy shit, I did!" The immediate crowd half moaned and half cheered and then demanded to see the ticket. To his better judgment, Cliff said, "No way dudes, this baby isn't leaving my sight." They all again groaned in disbelief and Cliff put the ticket in his tip bucket. His hands were shaking when he turned around as he tried to conceal his excitement and one of the guys at the bar said, "Look at ya, you're shakin' like a leaf. You must have hit something!" Cliff paused a second then calmly said, "Listen guys, keep this on the DL until I get it cashed. The last thing I need is somebody mugging me on my way home for a stupid lotto ticket." Another guy at the bar chimed in and said, "You wanna close up early and get out of here now? I'm sure Conrad would understand."

"No that's okay. I'll take a cab home and I wouldn't feel right closing early but seriously, everybody stay quiet at least until tomorrow. In fact, you guys behave a second while I run down and lock this in the office." Cliff said as he was turning and grabbing the ticket out of the bucket. He bound down the steps, opened the office, spun the lock on the safe quickly, tossed the ticket on the top shelf and locked it again. When he ran back upstairs he heard them all talking about how lucky he was. A fun job, lots of women, good looks and now a lotto winner! What an asshole. And so the jabs came for the next half hour while Cliff constantly reminded them to hush. There was no reason to bring any unwanted attention to the matter. He knew everybody in immediate company so he was wasn't worried but he definitely didn't want any of the strangers sparsely scattered around the bar to hear what was going on. He saw a twenty-dollar bill sitting on the bar under an empty beer bottle where Pauly had been. He looked around and asked openly, "Did Pauly leave?"

"Oh, he said goodbye, said he had another stop to make" came the general reply.

~

Rodney was hanging out with Jimmy on a stoop in The Bronx when Jimmy's cell phone rang. He picked it up, then stepped away insinuating an important call. He came back, looked at Rodney with a serious scowl on his face and said, "Lets go, we got some paper to collect."

CHAPTER FIVE

The Bronx is home to every walk of life and every kind of person. Rich, poor and every level in the middle. Black, white, yellow, red, brown and every shade in between. Young and old, families and broken homes, singles and newlyweds. Entire neighborhoods are often separated by a street or a park. One could argue that all of the people on the entire planet could likely be found to be represented in The Bronx. It also holds two different worlds separated by the skylight of the Sun or by the glow of street lamps and headlights. Crime is common in the poorer neighborhoods and the nighttime shadows made for plenty of cover.

There are very few skyscrapers in The Bronx. It is primarily made of buildings not climbing farther than six stories into the air. Many of the apartment buildings are brownstones and walk-ups much like those you see as the backdrop for the children's television show "Sesame Street." There are plenty of fast food restaurants and gas stations sprinkled throughout as well as some old neighborhood staples that are privately owned and fighting to stay afloat as Corporate America continues to try to take over. Pizza joints, diners, barber shops and a few bars where the staff hasn't changed in twenty years are part of the strength and stability that New Yorkers take pride in. As the majority of the streets are filled with people working and getting along without incident, it is impossible to have so many people in such a small area without conflict.

Most of the crime committed in The Bronx is handled at night. The daytime stuff was generally traffic related. Road rage is often and fights between private cars and taxicabs are quite common. Parking tickets are handed out constantly and cops could always catch somebody smoking weed in any of the parks if they needed an arrest. When it is dark outside, the issues to police become a whole other bag of problems. Domestic disturbance calls are answered constantly, especially in the housing projects. Alcohol, drugs, jealousy and lack of money make for sticky home lives for many of the folks living there. Theft is an every night occurrence. Muggings are reported several times a week, usually underground toward the end of the subway lines. Gunfire isn't nearly as common as it used to be, but is still a familiar sound. Marijuana and cocaine dealing are a common occupation for any male under 25, and Jimmy was one of the biggest in the area.

~

Jimmy and Rodney grew up in a housing project right in the middle of The Bronx. They rarely left the area, but if necessary, the 5-train was only a few blocks away and connected them to anywhere in the city they needed to be. Jimmy was only six weeks older than Rodney but was 60lbs. heavier. He was a big man of 23 years made mostly of muscle. He started lifting weights at a very young age because he learned early on that he would be fighting for most of his life because he was white. By the time he was fifteen years old, everybody in the area knew who he was. Not only did he stick out because he was white, but he was 6'3" tall and a helluva basketball player. Tough kids with muscles and an affinity for basketball earned quick respect with the neighborhood youngsters.

Rodney was far from big; it just wasn't in his biology. He'd lifted weights and ate like a horse through his entire adolescence but was never able to fill his clothes with any real size. He was a smart young man, raised by a single mother who pounded good grades into his head. She was also a bit passive, which rubbed off on Rodney, and he became the victim of bullies until Jimmy stepped in the picture.

~

They were 13 years old. Jimmy was always at the park, which was really just a fenced off concrete basketball court with a few benches on the sides, shooting baskets after school until an hour or so after dark. Many of the kids would work their way in and out of the pickup games as the nights wore on, but most never lasted more than an hour or two before wanting to do something else or head home for dinner. Rodney could see the park from the kitchen window so his mother allowed him to go over as long as she could see him and he was inside by dark. She would watch as she cooked dinner and cleaned around the kitchen. She ached as she saw her son just sit in the corner of the fence and watch the stronger kids play. He usually took homework with him to look busy, but none of it ever really got completed while at the park.

The other kids would call him Erkel or Four Eyes whenever the chance to be funny came up. He was never invited to play and he never asked to join.

He wasn't big enough and he wasn't athletic but admired those who were. At school, he kept to himself and endured the same abuse. He shared a science class with Jimmy and they were assigned to be partners on a lab one day. Rodney did most of the work but Jimmy was curious so he started asking questions, "Why don't you be playin with us at the park? I see you come over."

"I'm too small and I've never had much practice." Rodney replied quietly.

Jimmy pressed on, "Alright then but why you so quiet? How come you don't be talkin?"

"It's just easier not to." Rodney quipped.

"Alright man, sorry." Jimmy said and let it go. After the lab work was done and they gathered their books he thanked Rodney for his help and said, "See you at the park."

As they walked out of the classroom for lunch, Rodney got a shoulder check from one of the kids that was two years older and then slapped in the back of his head by another bully as he walked down the hall. It was a daily occurrence, Rodney was used to it, but Jimmy had never noticed, until that day.

After school the usual suspects were at the park playing basketball and Rodney, with his mothers' usual permission, walked over to sit and pretend to do homework. Jimmy gave Rodney a nod making him feel really cool for a second, a feeling he didn't often have. The coolness however, was short lived. The same two bullies who knocked him around on the way to lunch just happened to see him sitting in the park on the ground with his back against the fence as they walked down the street. They were rarely on this street and at 15 years old, hadn't quite learned the value of territory. They began to chuckle and point as they walked up behind Rodney, who hadn't noticed them yet. "Look yo, it's the nerdy nigga!" Barked one of the bullies.

The other chimed in, "HAAA Hey Erkel, why you in the park doin homework?"

Rodney didn't even turn around. He knew who was there by the voices. These boys had been terrorizing him for over a year. He felt the skin in his cheeks flushing as he didn't want to be embarrassed in front of the only guy that had said anything nice to him in weeks. He silently prayed that they would just keep walking by, say whatever you want, but keep walking. This wish of course, is not one often granted by 15-year old bullies. They stepped to the fence from the outside. One of them spit through it and the goober flew by Rodney's ear and landed on his math homework. The basketball stopped bouncing.

"Hey nerdy nigga, I'm talkin to you."

Rodney didn't move, he looked at his math homework. His heart was pumping fear through his body like a fire hydrant. His thoughts shifted from his new friend to his mother. *Was she looking out the window? Did she see this? Please don't let this happen in front of my Mom!*

"Yo punk-ass, you deaf?"

One of the bullies stepped back while the other turned to watch. He lined up as if he was a place kicker on a football team, took two steps and kicked the fence that Rodney's back was against and struck him directly in the spine of his lower back. The chain links rattled, he jolted forward, tears instantly streaming down his face. He quickly scootched forward a couple feet so he couldn't be kicked again with the protection of the fence. They would have to come inside the fenced-in playground to get another crack at him. *What a nightmare. Was Mom watching?* His thoughts stayed there.

He heard the rattle of the gate, which startled him. He turned expecting to see the bullies on their way in, but to his surprise, it was Jimmy and two other kids going out. Rodney stood up, shoved his papers under his arms and was trying to figure out the best way to run across the street and get home through his teary eyes and watery glasses. Everything seemed to go in slow motion for the next 20 seconds. Jimmy walked briskly towards the two punks and barked, "You motha-fuckas got a problem?"

"Yo fuck you Jimmy!" The older of the bullies said. And with that, Jimmy shot a chest pass into the kids face from less than 6 feet away, busting his nose and causing his eyes to water so quickly he couldn't see. Jimmy continued his stride, walked straight up to the second bully, grabbed his sweatshirt and slammed him to the ground with what seemed like zero effort. The other two basketball players stayed back about 3 feet while Jimmy worked his magic. He stepped on the head of the bully on the ground as he reached and grabbed the one who couldn't see by the neck of his sweatshirt. He jerked him hard so he was bent over and Jimmy's face was now in between the two troublemakers. He looked at both of them and snarled, "If either of you ever touch my boy Rodney again, I will bust you up every day until you graduate. Believe that's real." He released the first, stepped off the head of the second, picked up his basketball and returned to the court with his two buddies in tow. They started shooting up the ball again as if nothing happened. Rodney stood there for a moment while his enemies collected themselves and limped away. He turned to the guys on the court, who were focused on their game, then turned to the gate and walked across the street, completely confused as to what just went down.

The next day at school, Rodney approached Jimmy during science and quietly said, "Thanks a lot man, nobody has ever done anything like that for me before."

"Ain't nothin man. Come back over tonight and wear some sneakers, you gonna play ball with us from now on."

And with that simple encounter, Rodney and Jimmy became Rodney and Jimmy. One name was rarely said with the other. Rodney had what Jimmy didn't, and Jimmy had what Rodney didn't. They were inseparable.

~

Jimmy started selling marijuana when he was 14 years old. It was pretty simple, and he quickly became the number one dealer within a couple blocks of his apartment and the only one to speak of in his high school. He wasn't silly with his money, didn't flash it around or buy extravagant things and he didn't flash any real bling except for always having new sneakers on his feet. He also never used the drugs himself. He was a firm believer that one either sold or used, but if you did both, you were asking for trouble.

Jimmy was raised by his grandfather. His mother ran off soon after Jimmy was born and Jimmy never knew her. He suspected his grandfather talked to her from time to time on the phone but he never asked. It was strange enough dealing with being an unwanted accident. Grandpa's health had declined drastically in the final year of high school and he passed away just after Jimmy graduated. Since he was 18 years old at the time and a legal resident, he was able to keep the small two-bedroom apartment that he and his grandfather had lived in for over fifteen years.

He expanded into selling cocaine later that summer and the profits and money was coming quickly. He stashed it everywhere. Boxes, pictures, speakers, drawers and even books that he'd hollowed out held knot after knot of $100 bills. He started buying bigger quantities and in turn moving bigger quantities to some of the younger guys. By the time he was 23, he had gotten big enough that he rarely traveled around the city anymore. He had about 8 smaller dealers that he trusted that bought from him in bulk. He was planning to move to Florida and open a sports memorabilia shop when he turned 25. Cash out and live simple for the rest of his life.

While Jimmy built his little drug empire, Rodney was sticking to his mother's wishes. He stayed in school and attended Marymount Manhattan College and studied sociology. He planned to become a social worker for underprivileged children, but since he was so smart, Jimmy employed him to run a small sports book as well. He was in the clear legally, his hands were on nothing. Jimmy collected and paid out, he just needed Rodney to run the "office." Jimmy was connected with an online gambling site that charged a small fee for each account number that he needed. After three years, he had set up 160 accounts, all of which kept fairly active and the cash flow steady. Rodney handled the website and the spreadsheets, kept track of the accounts, and gave a Jimmy a list every Monday of who owed what and who needed to be paid. Rodney had an envelope waiting for him when he showed up every week. It was sealed and contained $800.00 in cash. It worked out to about 100 bucks for every 20 accounts per week. Not bad for about six hours of work.

Rodney kept another part time job to stay legit. He started working part time at The Foot Locker when he was 17 and had moved his way up to a part-time assistant manager now. He worked only about 20 hours a week, and again, he was mostly there for paperwork, computer skills, ordering, scheduling, and payroll. His brains were already paying off and with a Masters degree only 18 months away; he was looking forward to the years that lie ahead.

CHAPTER SIX

Detective Nelson stood in the doorway and shuffled his feet impatiently as he waited for the bloody cell phone to be delivered to him. There were flashes popping every few seconds as the detectives were diligently working their way around the pool table. The Coroner had arrived and was making his way toward Cliff to officially pronounce him dead. There were about twenty police officers standing around on the sidewalk whispering theories and waiting for orders. Conrad sat on the curb with his face buried in his hands, two cops standing next to him. The sun was coming up.

The flashes stopped for a moment and the phone was delivered. It was a flip phone and it was open. There was blood smudged on the screen and all over the keypad. Detective Nelson studied it for a moment afraid to touch a button that could allow blood to get under the keys and into the electronics, permanently taking it out of commission. He decided that since the blood had turned dark and seemed to have thickened that it was worth the risk. He touched the "enter" button and the screen lit up displaying the time and a picture of a dog. He then pushed "menu" and the option came up for "call history." He tapped down and again hit "enter" to see an outgoing call placed to somebody named "Jumper." He clicked "info" and the phone number to match Jumper popped up. He barked at an officer to take down the number. It was a California area code, which he hoped wouldn't create a problem given the time difference. He tapped talk and hoped he could get Jumper to pick up. He held the phone close to his ear without touching it to his face and waited for an answer. Four rings. No answer. Voicemail. A peppy voice came through the earpiece, "Yo, you've reached Jumper and I can't take your call but I'll get back atcha when I can." Detective Nelson spoke clearly in the direction of the mouthpiece and stated, "Jumper, this is Detective Nelson with the New York City Police Department. There has been an incident involving the owner of the phone I am calling from and you appear to be the last number that was dialed. It is of immediate importance that you call me as soon as you get this message. The number is 917-555-8080. Please waste no time as every second can make a difference this morning." He pulled the phone away and looked at it again before touching the "end" button.

The nearest officer, the one who took the phone number down, was standing just outside the door. Detective Nelson handed him a cell phone from his pocket and instructed him to dial Jumper's number over and over again for at least ten minutes with hopes that it he was sleeping and the ring would wake him. "Do NOT leave a message; in case his inbox is full

I don't want to bump out any messages possibly left by Cliff. Just let it ring 3 times, hang up and dial back." Nelson was quick and clear with his instructions. The officer stayed close and went to work.

~

Julian Jumper went to the University of Montana on a basketball scholarship. He was relatively short for collegiate basketball, only standing 6'2" but he was as quick as a rabbit and could jump like a kangaroo. He often dunked over guys standing 6'6" or taller, making his last name a favorite headline for the local newspapers. He was the most entertaining player on the team to watch.

Cliff exercised at the schools athletic complex at least four times a week. Julian worked his freshman year at the desk checking people's ID's for three hours on Monday, Wednesday, and Friday afternoons. As Cliff was checking in and chatting with Julian one day, he learned that he'd come to play basketball from Indianapolis. He didn't do much other than study, practice, and workout so Cliff invited him to go snowboarding on the next available Sunday. A new friendship was born.

Jumper, his last name being the moniker that everybody used, professors included, seemed to fit in anywhere he went. He always carried a smile and a happy laugh that was contagious. Cliff introduced him around the entire town, and many of the townsfolk enjoyed meeting and chatting with the local basketball celebrity. He went to dinners with Cliff and Calvin at their mother's, their father's and even spent a Thanksgiving with them at the grandparents a year when all the flights were grounded due to a blizzard in Indianapolis. By the time Cliff and Jumper graduated, they were as tight as any two friends could be.

After graduation, Jumper took a job teaching elementary school and coaching high school basketball in Mission Viejo, California, a town in the southernmost part of the Los Angeles area. He and Cliff still talked three or four times a month and tried to see each other twice a year. Living on opposite coasts didn't seem to get in the way of keeping the friendship in tact.

~

Conrad, still balled up and sitting on the curb, snapped his head up as if he was startled from a nightmare. "Dammit!" He hollered in the direction of Detective Nelson. "Let's get in the office and look at the security videos!"

"You have security cameras in this place?" Detective Nelson asked with surprise.

"Yeah, had them installed about four months ago when all those purses were getting snatched around the neighborhood." Conrad was already getting to his feet.

"Well that's a bit of information I could've used a half hour ago."

"Oh shut up Nelson and come with me."

They walked around the corner of the bar to the side entrance that leads to the basement. Neither Conrad nor Nelson wanted to see Cliff's body again and the detectives were still busy all over the bar. Conrad dug into his pockets and found his keys. He stuck a gold colored key into the lock of the gate that was protecting the stairs. A silver one unlocked the door at the bottom of the steps before entering the dingy basement. A minute later they were at the door to the office, which had a detective dusting for prints around the doorknob and snapping pictures of the smudged footprint on the door. The key didn't turn as easy as usual, probably because the lock was a little bent from being kicked, but it still turned. After confirming they could touch the doorknob without disturbing evidence, they entered the office. Conrad sat at the desk and Nelson stood behind him as he punched a couple keys and buttons triggering the monitor to turn on. The cameras were still on, and several angles of the bar were showing the bustling activity that was taking place right above them, an investigation fully underway. Conrad reached over and closed the office door and then he pulled up the recorded history for the last 6 hours. They had estimated Cliff's fight was right around closing time, 4:00 a.m.

Just as Conrad was narrowing down the precise time slots necessary and jostling which camera angles were going give the best views, Detective Nelson put his hand on his shoulder and said, "Conrad, if you don't wanna watch this, its okay. I can go through it myself or with my tech guy so you don't have to see this."

"Piss on that." Conrad said with the gruff of an old sailor. "I wanna see these bastards myself."

Conrad was already passed the shock and sadness. Now he was angry and wanted justice. He'd been through too much in his life to dwell on such things for too long, it didn't get anything accomplished. Detective Nelson was called upon from outside of the office so he opened the door and had a quick conversation with an officer who informed him that the press had arrived. While his attention was away, Conrad quickly hit a copy and save command to another hard drive so that he would have his own copy of the evenings events. He knew they were going to confiscate this video because it was evidence and he'd never see it again if he didn't save his own copy.

All at once the copy was completed, two thugs were on the screen walking in the door of the bar and Detective Nelson had returned his attention to the security tapes.

Not bad computer skills for an old man. Conrad thought.

~

Jumper woke up at 6:30 a.m. Since school was out for a couple more weeks, he ran a basketball camp from 9:00 to 11:30 in the mornings. He liked to get up early and get an hour of exercise in before heading off to supervise and coach the camp kids. He looked at the ceiling for a minute and then swung his feet over the edge of the bed to rev up the day. He rubbed his ankles then lifted his rear off the bed to stretch hamstrings. He held that position for about 30 seconds before slowly rolling his entire body upright into what looked like a "Y" capped off with an open mouth and a glorious yawn. Wake up ritual complete, time for a shower!

He lumbered toward the bedroom door and noticed that his cell phone on the top of his dresser was trying to get his attention. The tiny little indicator light was popping like a beacon every 10 seconds letting Jumper know that he had missed some sort of activity during his slumber. He snatched it up, disconnected its power source, and flipped it open as he continued moving toward the bathroom. He stopped in the hallway, mumbling what he read on the screen, "37 missed calls, 2 new voicemails." He no longer had to pee. He passed the bathroom and went to the kitchen table and sat down. The call history showed that the first two calls came from Cliff and the remaining 35 were from a number, all the same, he didn't recognize. The times on the calls from Cliff were 2 hours apart and the following 35 immediately following Cliff's second attempt. His heartbeat seemed to double as he punched the button to listen to his voicemails.

~

Detective Nelson was now passed the 24-hour mark without sleep. It was 10:07 in the morning on the east coast. He was sitting in front of a screen at his office watching the security videos that he had indeed confiscated from Conrad and The Tan Hat Man. He had placed both his personal cell phone and Cliff's cell phone on his desk while waiting to hear from Jumper. Nelson's cell phone suddenly erupted with vibration and he jerked to see who was calling. The California number was on the screen so Nelson flipped it open and went to work, barking, "Detective Nelson."

"Yes hello, my name is Julian Jumper. I received a message from you expressing an urgent return call. I apologize for the delay as I sleep with my ringer silenced. What do you need?"

"Hi Julian. Thank you for getting back to me. Did you receive a message from Cliff Barry last night?"

"No sir. However, my call history shows that he tried to call two times. What's going on?"

"What is the nature of your relationship with Cliff?"

"He's my best friend. Went to college together and we're still close. Is he okay?"

"Actually no Julian. Unfortunately, Cliff was the victim of what appears to be a homicide last night and you were the last call made from his phone. Are you in New York?"

There was a pause for a moment. Jumper had already feared the worst because of the message he *did* receive from Cliff, but it was a personal message and didn't feel it necessary to reveal its contents to the detective, at least not yet.

"No Detective, I'm in Mission Viejo, California. Is he really dead? Cliff Barry? Bartender? Good looking guy from Montana?"

"I'm afraid so." The detective said quietly.

"I'll be on the next flight to New York."

"Call me when you've arrived."

CHAPTER SEVEN

Rodney hated tagging along when Jimmy had "tough guy" business to handle. When he was younger, he admired watching Jimmy get whatever he needed with just raw intimidation, something Rodney never possessed. He was older now and it all just seemed silly. Jimmy never expected Rodney to get involved in any capacity except to be present and watch his back.

Jimmy had a Honda Civic that he'd paid cash for when he was 20 years old. It was used when he bought it but in great condition. It didn't have anything flashy to draw attention to it, no big spinning rims, no tinted windows or colored lights, just a factory made Honda Civic that an old man had driven until he couldn't pass his driving test any longer. It was ideal for anything Jimmy needed it for.

Jimmy and Rodney jumped in the Civic and started towards Manhattan. Rodney was looking out of the window with his mind on school when Jimmy broke the silence.

"I don't know how this is going to go down."

"Why?" Rodney inquired. "What is this about?"

"This kid has a winning scratch off lotto ticket and I'm supposed to take it from him."

"What? Yo, we ain't into mugging fools. Why we gotta take it?"

"Pauly asked me too." Jimmy said with an exhale.

"What the fuck man? Why you still do shit for that dude? You on your own now right?" Snapped Rodney, clearly irritated.

"Yeah but only cuz they let me. The families still exist man. I do a couple favors a year for them and they leave me alone. Only two more years anyways, then I be in Florida."

"I don't want nothing to do with no muggin man, I'm gonna wait in the car. Where this kid at?"

"He's in a bar." Jimmy said.

"Cool, just go in, get a beer, wait til he hits the bathroom and go in and take it from him. I'll wait. He's probably drunk and talkin shit anyway, that's how Pauly found out."

"Come with me yo, it ain't that easy."

Why not?" Rodney asked.

"Because he's the bartender."

"Aw fuck that man, can't you just tell Pauly he was never alone? I gotta work tomorrow; I can't be up all night waitin for this cat to get off work."

"We'll just go in and check it out. Pauly said its dead and no bouncer. If it's empty, it'll be easy. If there is a bunch of people, you take the car and I'll wait it out and get the train back."

"Alright man but I don't like this, you don't need this shit. How much is the stupid thing worth?"

"I don't know."

~

The Honda Civic pulled into a metered parking space about 10 blocks from The Tan Hat Man. Rodney and Jimmy got out and closed the doors. Jimmy never wore a hat when he drove, as it was just another reason for a cop to form an opinion of him and pull him over for nothing. He put his oversized fitted Yankee hat on backward, hit a button on his keychain to make the car chirp, and strode up the sidewalk with Rodney. At 2:20 a.m., after the half-mile stroll, they entered The Tan Hat Man.

~

Cliff was in the corner of the bar wiping off some bottles. No customers at the tables and only three guys sitting at the bar chatting when Rodney and Jimmy walked in. Everybody took a quick glance at the two new customers but since nobody knew them, they turned back to their beer and conversations. The door to the men's room swung open as Rodney and Jimmy settled into two stools at the bar. They both looked and saw a fat guy with a red face waddle out of the restroom, straight passed them and toward the exit with his hand in the air waving goodbye.

"Later Red!" Cliff hollered in the general direction of the door.

Jimmy and Rodney both chuckled at the irony amongst themselves. Cliff approached them and said, "What can I get you fellas?"

"Two Corona." Jimmy answered as he put a twenty on the bar.

They pushed their limes through the hole and into the neck of the bottles as Cliff made change for the drinks. Jimmy took a quick mental inventory of Cliff, realizing he was just as big, about the same age, and probably had lifted as many weights. *I hope this dude don't put up a fight.* Jimmy thought. He and Rodney sat quietly and looked at the TV's showing the late night edition of Sports Center as Cliff returned to his cleaning.

During the next ten minutes, two more customers had cleared their checks, left a tip and said goodbye. The only person left at the bar was an Italian guy in his 50's with a narrow silver mustache that didn't even reach the corners of his mouth. He was chuckling in a quiet private conversation with Cliff. There was money on the bar in front of him so Jimmy was hoping he'd hurry up and leave. He wanted to get this over and out of the way. He hated when he had to do "muscle" work.

Another minute passed and Cliff leaned over the bar and gave the Italian a hug. Goodbyes and more chuckles were exchanged. The door was closing and the current song was ending. An eerie silence fell over the bar. Rodney stood up and walked toward the bathroom. Cliff walked over to Jimmy whose beer bottle only had a lime in it and asked, "You ready for another?"

"Nah man. I'm gonna wait for my boy to get out of the bathroom, get that lotto ticket from you, then we gonna leave."

There was a pause as this information registered in Cliff's mind. Then he looked Jimmy dead in the eye and said, "Excuse me?"

Jimmy actually shifted his weight to the other foot, showing a discomfort he rarely felt. Nobody ever looked Jimmy directly in the eye when there was a confrontation. He was too big and too mean and most people didn't have the confidence or ability to look directly into his eyes. Even the tough guys who tried were actually looking at his chin, but never the eyes. Jimmy was thrown off. *Too late to turn back now.*

"Look," Jimmy growled, looking straight back at him. "I'm here to collect a lotto ticket from you. Now you either gonna give it to me or I'm gonna take it, but either way, I'm walking out of there with it."

"Ticket is gone bro. The old guy that just left took it with him for safe keeping."

Jimmy leaned over the bar, his lip was now quivering with anger, and quietly spoke, "It's in the office. I know it's in the office, so this conversation is over." The door to the bathroom opened up and

Rodney stopped, knowing that the ice had been broken.

A million things went through Cliff's mind in less than five seconds. *Fuckin' Pauly! I never trusted that bastard! I know it was him. Can I take this dude? I'll knock the skinny kid out with one shot! Where is the gun? There has to be a gun somewhere? Does the skinny kid have it? If I give them the ticket, can I just call the cops, they arrest him and I get it back? Probably not, it'll change hands five times by noon tomorrow and 6 months from now some old guy upstate will cash it and it'll never be traced. Are they gonna kill me after I give it to them? If I fight, I have a chance. If I give it to them, they'll kill me in the office for sure and the cameras can't see me down there. Where is the fucking gun? You can't rob somebody without a gun, can you? Where is my phone? No chance I can get a 911 call out right now. Where is the gun? If I fight, I have to strike first! Dumb bastard is leaning over the bar. Big mistake. Chicken shit in the bathroom is scared to death. I like my odds. Where's the gun? Fuck it, here we go!*

"Lets dance." Cliff barked, and buried his forehead into Jimmy's snarling face.

~

Cliff and Calvin, like most brothers, grew up fighting in the backyard. They would wrestle like Hulk Hogan or box like Mike Tyson. Sometimes they would combine the two and have Hulk Hogan versus Mike Tyson matches! They never tried to actually hurt each other, but they always went full bore, so much so that Dad bought them boxing gloves for Christmas one year to try to slow down the brutality. Bloody noses and lips and cuts and bruises were usually when the fights stopped. Mom was the referee that usually had to come out of the house and put an end to it, though she always let her boys be boys.

They had to quit being so rough in the teen years since Cliff was hitting puberty. He was just getting too strong for Calvin and both parents agreed they needed to keep things fair. They joined the only boxing club in Missoula called Jake's Gloves. It was a small gym with only 80 members of all ages. They had the basics; speed bags, heavy bags, jump ropes, a small weight area, a wrestling mat and two boxing rings. There was sparring all the time, always done by weight and always with full protective headgear and mouthpieces. Jake was always around and supervising, giving tips and showing technique. He had been a golden glove champion 15 years earlier so everyone went to him for their boxing needs.

Cliff and Calvin loved Jake's. They were there almost every day for their workouts. Once Calvin caught up to Cliff in weight, they began boxing each other again. They even covered for Jake one week every summer so he could take a vacation without closing the gym. Their skills were sharp, and though neither Barry boy wanted to pursue it competitively, either of them could have.

~

Cliff grabbed a bottle from the speed rack and chucked it towards the bathroom hoping it would make the skinny kid go back inside. All in one motion, he hopped over the bar as the bottle shattered on the brick wall next to the men's room door. Jimmy couldn't see; his eyes were welled up with tears. The first sign of blood was visible, both on top of his nose where the skin had broken and from the nostrils. Just as Jimmy was standing up to retaliate, Cliff had shoved both hands into his chest tossing him back and into a table. It toppled over and Jimmy went down with it. He quickly rolled over and pushed himself up only to be kicked down again. Cliff then picked up a stool and swung it like a sledgehammer into Jimmy's ribs. He turned and looked for Rodney, who was not visible, so Cliff assumed he went back into the bathroom. He moved quickly toward the end of the bar where the phone was. Before he could get there he erupted in anger screaming at the ceiling, "FUCK, I HATE THIS! YOU DUMB FUCKS!"

Cliff picked up the phone and turned around to make sure Jimmy was still down. He saw a flash, then an instant of blackness. He was knocked out for only about 2 seconds; enough time for the phone to fall on the floor. He put his hand to his face and looked to his right. Rodney had swung a pool cue at him like a baseball bat with the fat end striking him square in the mouth. His lips were busted all to hell. Jimmy was getting to his feet, blood drenching the front of his sweatshirt. The sound system was next to the phone. Cliff reached and spun the volume up as loud as it would go. *Maybe a passerby will hear it. Maybe the neighbors will hear it. And these two won't be able to communicate.* Then he charged right back up to Jimmy who now had his eyes clear and could see so the real fight began. Rodney smartly stood back and watched in disbelief as these two rough necks squared off. They were both screaming at each other, but none of it was audible since Cliff cranked the music. Cliff kept hitting Jimmy with a jab in his nose, trying to just work it, get it open, make his eyes water, get him to back down. *Anything to put an end to this.* After the fourth straight shot to the nose Jimmy lunged low and the two of them hit the ground. He pulled back and finally got a punch to land. It hit Cliff hard and square in the mouth and again Cliff saw the flash. *Shit! Two shots, two bolts! I gotta get on my feet!* He tried to roll over but the hits were coming with a flurry and the floor was slippery. He tried to lean up between shots but they were coming too quick. He finally just started punching back until one connected and he was able to get out from under Jimmy.

There was a very short pause. Both monsters were on their behinds and Rodney was behind the pool table. Cliff and Jimmy locked eyes again and Cliff knew this wasn't over. He popped up, grabbed a stool and chucked it at Jimmy. He fended it off with his forearm and grabbed the small table next to him, spinning quickly and throwing the table at Cliff. He tried to move but the legs of the table swung weirdly and hit him in the knee with such force that he buckled over in pain. Jimmy then grabbed the empty Corona bottle on the bar, smashed against the bar to create a sharp edge; walked up to Cliff and yanked his head back, putting the glass to his neck. He started to guide and walk the limping Cliff toward the steps to the basement when Cliff dropped and spun and hit Jimmy in the same spot in the ribs that he'd buried the bar stool early. Jimmy dropped the glass and winced in pain, but it wasn't enough. He brought his knee up blasting Cliff in the face. Blood was now flying everywhere, with every blow that each one delivered. Cliff tried to stand but his knee gave out again. Jimmy tipped another table over on Cliff, the side of it shattering his ankle. That leg was now completely useless. The next 30 seconds was just a rage-induced barrage of violence. Cliff was on the ground, bleeding, broken and defenseless. Jimmy grabbed a pool cue and swung it hard several times until it broke in half over Cliff's ribs. He threw tables around. Screaming at nothing, he grabbed a pool ball off the table and hurled it into the mirrors behind the bar. His final blow was with a stool. He picked it straight up in the air and slammed it right back down. One of the legs crushed Cliff on the cheekbone and tore the flesh back so far that if it weren't for the blood, teeth would have been visible. A pause, a breath, and then he lumbered toward the steps.

Rodney was freaking out. He ran down the steps behind Jimmy repeating over and over, "What the fuck Jimmy? What the fuck?" The two of them arrived at the door. There were three locks on it and the frame had obviously been reinforced. Jimmy instantly realized there was no way they were getting inside the office without the proper keys, and they surely didn't have time to go digging around the bar for the bartenders keys. He kicked it three times with almost no result, looked around in defeat, and headed back up the steps with Rodney in tow.

When they reached the top, they tried to communicate but the music was still blaring, so Jimmy waved Rodney to follow. At the door, Jimmy paused, looked outside to find an empty street, and then quickly opened the door for him and Rodney to exit. He pushed it closed to hide the noise then tore off his sweatshirt. They started walking down the street as Jimmy dabbed his face with his sweatshirt. Five minutes later, they were in the car in silence, both trying to figure out what just happened.

~

Cliff regained consciousness when the touch of fresh air that found its way into the bar, during the exit of Rodney and Jimmy, finally brushed his face. It almost felt like the kiss of an angel. He went to open his eyes but realized they were open. He moved his arm to his face to wipe them out. He realized only one eye still worked. The final blow that Jimmy delivered with the stool when Cliff was knocked out basically disconnected his eye from his brain. He went to sit up but couldn't. He tried to move his legs but only one moved. He tried to use his other hand but had no control over his fingers. He realized he had one eye, one hand, and since he could hear the music, at least one ear. Then he realized something else, nothing hurt. He felt no pain. He remembered the brutal fight he just had and knew he was busted up, but no pain? *I'm dying, that's the only explanation.*

Cliff took his good arm and hand and reached around to his back pocket where he always kept his cell phone. He was able to find his pocket and fish his cell phone out. He brought it back around to his face and with the working eye, checked to see if it was still usable. He pushed a button, it lit up, and he was ready to make his last call. He flipped the phone open and punched the button for "contacts." He tapped the letter "J" on his keypad, which took him to that section of the phone book. Six clicks down and he arrived at "Jumper." Now he just had to wait until the current song ended and time his call in between songs. Since the jukebox was easily 20 years old, it usually took about 45 seconds to switch tracks. He pushed talk while the current song was winding down. Jumper was asleep and it would ring four times before voicemail got involved. His timing was perfect. The song ended and the beep in the earpiece signifying the leaving of the message all happened at once. It was time for Cliff's final words.

CHAPTER EIGHT

Shuffling feet. Luggage bumping around. A monotone voice over the intercom. A baby crying. The wrapper of a sandwich being crumpled. Monotonous chatter. The beep of an airport vehicle crawling through the masses. It all sounded like it was being piped into Jumpers ear through a funnel as he sat in a chair at the crowded gate of JFK's international airport while waiting for the arrival of the Barry family. It had been far too long since he'd seen them, and these were not the circumstances he had anticipated for their reunion. His plane had arrived two hours prior so he just figured he'd hang back and they'd all head into the city together.

As he watched the plane crawl into its place at the gate, anxiety rushed through his body and a frog suddenly jumped into his throat. He had hoped he would be able to avoid emotion when they came out of the gate, but he now knew that tears were inevitable. He stood up and faced the gate as the first people came into view, then the bold frame of Calvin. The two young men locked up with a hug that would take a crowbar to separate as Sally took her place to the side. Just as Calvin and Jumper were loosening up, Cliff and Calvin's parents spilled out of the gate for more tears and more hugs. Not a word had been spoken and the reunion had already lasted more than two minutes.

The five of them turned away from the gate and headed toward the center walkway before Mr. Barry finally broke the ice.

"You been here long Jumper?"

"No, only about two hours. I didn't have any reason to rush into the city so I assumed you wouldn't mind riding in together."

"Of course!" Ms. Barry hurriedly replied through a sniffle. "I'm very happy you waited for us."

After following a sign that pointed to baggage claim and transportation, Jumper and the Barry family walked by a television monitor that was carrying a scene that made them all stop in their tracks. Two men were being put into a squad car with their hands cuffed behind them and the closed caption explained that they were "arrested and charged with the murder of Cliff Barry, a Manhattan bartender, after several calls came in following the broadcast of their pictures taken from a security camera inside The Tan Hat Man on the Upper East Side." A picture of Cliff popped up in the corner of the screen and tears erupted from the eyes of Jumper and all four Barry's.

"Damn, they already got em," Calvin said, sort of off to nobody.

~

Detective Nelson had watched the video several times and had several frames to choose from to make a still shot that the news could air in hopes of catching Jimmy and Rodney. He chose one still of each of them, hoping they were clear enough and showed enough character for somebody to recognize them and call in a tip. The photos were released as "breaking news" during the lunch hour on all the local news feeds. Within five minutes, they had already received over 30 calls, and had over 100 calls by 1:00. Every call was quick and simple, naming Jimmy and Rodney and a short theory as to where they could probably be found. A few asked if there was a reward for making the call. There wasn't.

Jimmy and Rodney were sitting in Jimmy's apartment when the news broke. They had been awake all morning discussing what their next move was to be. They were planning to wait until the evening news to see if any information was released and could link them to the murder. They were shocked when the pictures flashed on the screen at noon. The silence was broken by a blast of both cell phones screaming almost simultaneously. Neither one answered. Rodney began to breathe strangely. Jimmy looked at him and said with a rare degree of tenderness, "Yo, they gonna be here in a few minutes. No point leavin. It's on me homeboy, you gonna be alright. Just tell them you didn't know nothing, were just out for a drink with me. Aaiight?"

"Yeah," Rodney barely squeaked.

They stood up and hugged for a moment before Jimmy left the room as Rodney sat down with tears streaming down his face. *What is my mother gonna do?*

The cops got there within 20 minutes of the initial broadcast. As both young men were coming out in cuffs, a couple of news crews were shouting questions and pointing cameras. The footage would run with the story for the rest of the afternoon and through the evening. The New York Post and The Daily News would make their mug-shots front-page news tomorrow.

~

The sun was going down. Mr. Barry had rented an SUV to have while in the city. As most Montana men, he was set in his ways, wanted to do his own driving and didn't wish to rely on cabs, buses, or subway trains. The ride in was quiet, no radio and little conversation. Jumper looked out of the left window while Calvin looked out the right. Sally sat between them and Ms. Barry was buckled into the front passenger seat. They followed the signs to New York City and soon crossed onto Manhattan via the 59th Street Bridge.

Traffic was slow moving. One-way streets everywhere. No turns on red lights. Horns blaring constantly. No speed limit signs. *How the hell do I know if I'm doing something wrong?* Thought Mr. Barry, but kept his frustrations quiet. After maneuvering to the center of the island, he finally found the Hyatt he had booked on 42nd Street and Park Avenue earlier that morning. They unloaded the SUV in front of the hotel and sent the car off with the valet. Mr. Barry, Calvin and Jumper shared one suite while Sally and Ms. Barry took another. They decided to shower and meet in the lobby in an hour. It was time to have dinner and map out a plan for the coming days.

~

Katy woke up in London to get ready for her red-eye return trip home. She logged on to her laptop and pulled up her Facebook page. She sat in shock as she read her "wall."

"Are you okay?"

"I'm so sorry to hear about Cliff!"

"My heart goes out to you, Cliff, his family and everyone lucky enough to have known him" were the first messages she read before slamming her computer shut and digging out her phone. She tried to call Cliff's phone but it only went to voicemail. She then called one of her roommates only to confirm the news. It felt like somebody shot a gaping hole right through her stomach. She couldn't move.

She was supposed to check into the airport for her flight back in two hours. After sitting for what seemed forever, she finally got into the shower. She was wondering how to handle work. Could she actually keep her head enough and fight back tears to work through her flight back to New York? Even if she called off and got a substitute, she'd probably be flying back on the same flight that she was supposed to work anyway; and only if there was an available seat. She decided she would do her best to work through the shift. At least she was sure to make it back that way. Just as she was getting out of the shower, there was a knock at the door.

"Who's there?" Katy asked.

"It's me, Jolene," was the reply from the fellow flight attendant. Katy opened the door and Jolene threw her arms around her in a solid embrace. Katy instantly welled up with tears. They hugged for over a minute and Katy turned to grab some tissue from the bathroom.

"Are you gonna work this morning or sit passenger?" asked Jolene.

"I'm gonna work it, try to keep my mind busy til I get home."

"Good. Don't worry about it, we'll all cover for you. I'm gonna finish getting dressed and I'll come back to get you before we catch our shuttle. Is that okay?"

"That's perfect," sniffled Katy. "Thank you." The door closed behind Jolene and Katy returned to getting ready before heading off to work.

CHAPTER NINE

Jumper freshened up quickly and went to the lobby to wait for the rest of the family. He looked at the little advertisement stand and quickly saw a card for a bar/restaurant called The Public House that was only a few blocks from the hotel. He snatched it up and sat on a comfortable sofa while he waited. His thoughts wouldn't leave the voicemail. He had no idea how or when to let the family hear it or how they would react. Every time he thought of it, a massive frog jumped in his throat as he constantly tried to fight back tears. It was just so Cliff, so calm in the worst of situations, keeping his head and leaving instructions for his best friend to be carried out with a delicate touch that Jumper was now required to deliver.

The elevator door opened and the family stepped into the lobby as Jumper stood up. Calvin suggested asking the concierge for a close place to eat. Jumper held out the flier he'd grabbed and said, "The picture looks like it has big booths." The simplicity of his reasoning caused the first chuckle since the reunion and the decision was made. After getting directions from a baggage handler at the front door, the five of them stepped out of the hotel and headed toward The Public House on foot.

It was indeed only a few minutes away. Upon arrival, the place looked like it was winding down from a busy evening. It was 9:15 p.m. Most of the tables had been cleared and reset. The hostess placed them in a huge booth in the corner that comfortably fit all five of them. There were several employees busy behind the bar and around the restaurant cleaning and handling the remainder of the nightly duties. A gorgeous little waitress approached the table and took the drink and appetizer order. Three waters, a Diet Coke for Mr. Barry, and a draft beer for Calvin sent the waitress away, clearly a little bummed that this was not a "drinking" table. The menus were opened but nobody was really looking, appetites were scarce. The waitress returned, delivered the drinks and took the order. A couple appetizers for the table and a cup of soup for Ms. Barry was the order.

After the menus were collected, Mr. Barry looked around the table and asked, "What is our plan of action?"

"Has anybody called the detective yet?" Jumper asked.
The consensus was no, so Mr. Barry volunteered to make that call after dinner. Calvin looked across the table at Jumper and asked, "Who called you this morning? How did you know about all of this?"

Jumper's heart skipped a beat because he was not going to lie to the family, but he wasn't ready to deliver the message yet. "The detective actually, he said my phone number was the last call placed from

Cliff's phone so he called to see who I was and if I'd heard or knew anything."

The answer was sufficient; the table was quiet again for a moment. Sips of drinks were taken. Finally, Calvin couldn't hold it in. "I'm gonna kill the mother fucker that did this."

"Calvin!" Ms. Barry said sternly in her best motherly watch-your-tongue tone.

"Well dammit Mom, we don't know anything! Why would anybody hurt Cliff? I just talked to him yesterday. He was happy as ever! I can't sit back and just allow this."

Mr. Barry comforted, "I know son, I'm angry as well. We all saw the news, they already have the guys in custody. If they got the right ones, they'll be in prison for the rest of their lives hopefully."

"If he ever gets out..." Calvin said off to nobody and let the others complete the sentence in their own minds. Sally put her hand on Calvin's knee and the table went quiet again.

The appetizers and soup arrived and the waitress disappeared. A busboy popped in to top off any water that had been consumed. Everybody picked at the plates and slowly ate a couple bites in silence.

~

Detective Nelson was in his office when his phone rang. He'd gone home for a short bit and got a couple hours of sleep while the family was in the air. He was reviewing the security video again, trying to find a clue that would point to a reason that all of this had occurred. He was scheduled to interrogate Jimmy and Rodney and hoped that they would simply give him the answer. He saw Cliff go downstairs with something in his hand but he couldn't figure out what it was. The camera angles didn't give an angle showing the young girl scratch off the lotto ticket. His cell phone erupted from his desk. He picked up the phone, "Detective Nelson."

"Hello Detective, this is Cliff Barry's father."

"Have you arrived in New York?"

"Yes sir, the entire family is here, we're staying at the Hyatt on 42nd Street."

"Okay, let's plan to meet at 9:00 in the morning at my office. We have security tapes showing the events of last night and we've already arrested the suspects."

"Yes, we saw the news at the airport."

"I'm really sorry Mr. Barry, I will do everything in my power to make sure justice is served."

"I appreciate that Detective."

Mr. Barry wrote down the directions to the precinct and hung up his phone. He looked at Jumper and Calvin and said, "I'm gonna go for a walk, you guys wanna join?"

"Yes." They both said in unison.

"Calvin, call the other room. See if Sally and your mother would like to join."

They met in the hallway and headed out of the hotel together. The clouds lingering over the city was reflecting the glow of Times Square. They decided to head towards the light and walk off some steam.

~

When Katy arrived at JFK Airport the following morning, it was still dark outside. She fired a text message to Sally, the only phone number she had, and hoped that she would get a reply soon after the sun came up. Another flight attendant with a car dropped her off at her apartment. She got out of her work attire and into some pajamas, turned on the television, and watched some mindless syndicated comedy while lying in her bed with her eyes pooled in tears.

CHAPTER TEN

Both rooms had wake up calls set for 7:00 a.m. It was completely unnecessary since everybody was up long before the phone rang. Jumper had already showered and walked down to the nearest Starbucks and retrieved five cups of coffee. When he returned, Calvin walked next door to deliver two of them to the ladies. Sally was on the phone with Katy. She was explaining what they knew up to this point and let her know of the meeting at the precinct. There was a diner around the corner from the station, so Katy recommended that they meet there. It was a plan.

~

Detective Nelson was in his office at the break of dawn. He hated these days. He hated this part of his job. He was an excellent detective and took great pride in fighting crime, but wherever there is crime, there is a victim. Often it didn't bother him when the victim was mixed up in something he or she shouldn't be involved in. The majority of his cases involved thugs battling other thugs or women involved with the wrong kind of men, but on occasion an innocent party is in the wrong place at the wrong time and it seemed impossible to make sense of it all. He'd hoped it would get easier with time but it wasn't. It was as hard now as it was the first time he had to do it. This was even a little more difficult because he knew the victim. He could only imagine that the Barry family was wonderful, and he prayed that nothing turned up that proved Cliff was involved in something he shouldn't be.

A buzz came from his desk phone and a pleasant voice called to Detective Nelson. He replied, "Yeah?"

The receptionist said, "There is a Conrad and a Pedro here to see you."

"Send them in."

The Detectives office was cramped. It had a desk covered in paperwork and a computer screen on the corner facing his chair. There were two chairs directly on the other side of the desk and a tall, fake, cheap plant sitting in the corner next to the blinds that covered the two large windows. A tap at the door and the secretary opened it presenting Conrad and Pedro. They stepped inside, exchanged handshakes and good mornings, and took a seat across from the desk as Detective Nelson sat down on his side.

"Well, this seems like its pretty open and closed, but we still don't have a reason why this had to happen. I'm questioning the suspects later this afternoon. Do either of you have any idea what may have caused this?"

Conrad leaned forward and tried to play dumb, as if he hadn't watched the video twenty times himself, "Can you show me the security video again so that I can see who was in the bar before the fight?"

"Of course, I looked and I think I recognized Pauly from one of the angles, but it will be good for you to confirm it. I haven't seen him in over a year so I'm not sure. Is he still running his sports book?"

Conrad confirmed, "Yes. I don't see him often, more during the football season as some of the guys still like to put a little something on the games."

"Was Cliff a gambler?"

"Nope." Replied Conrad. "In fact, he couldn't stand Pauly. He is a loudmouth, and Cliff didn't like seeing people gamble on the games because he couldn't stand people hollering at the TV's and making asses of themselves with teams they could care less about. Some of these guys get a little too emotional."

"Well that's good to know. I couldn't make out any of the other people at the bar, but I'm sure you'll know who they are. Let's wait until after we've met with the family and then you and I can review the surveillance." Detective Nelson said as he was standing up. "Let's move into the conference room so we have plenty of room and fresh coffee. The Barry family should be here by 9:00."

As they all were standing up, Pedro quietly spoke, "Detective Nelson, my wife is in the waiting area. Do you mind if she joins us?"

"Of course not, I'll have her sent back."

Detective Nelson punched a button on the phone and ordered the receptionist to bring Reina to the conference room.

~

Katy was waiting in a large booth close to the door in the diner when she saw a cab stop in front. Jumper and Mr. Barry got out while a second cab pulled up directly behind them emptying the other three members of the party. She stood up and met Jumper at the door, giving him a massive hug while Mr. Barry stood on the street and gathered the rest of the family. She greeted all of them with massive hugs and tears. Ms. Barry said with a rasp, "It is so nice to finally meet you in person." And more tears from all of the ladies followed. When the embraces were finally through, they headed into the diner, and back to the large booth Katy had originally planted herself in.

Sally and Katy sipped water while Jumper had a large glass of fresh Orange Juice. Mr. and Ms. Barry ordered a cup of coffee, as did Calvin. They sat and discussed how nice it was to have everybody together and moved on to where in the world, literally, Katy was when she got word. After that story concluded, a time was checked, a twenty was thrown on the table, and they left the diner with seven minutes to find the precinct.

A short walk halfway up the block and they had arrived and entered into the local law enforcement headquarters. The receptionist, who was clearly anticipating their arrival, greeted them and then walked them down a hall and around a corner into the office break room, which doubled as a conference room when needed. It had the smell of fresh coffee and a plate of doughnuts and bagels was sitting on a counter. Detective Nelson asked to put the "Do Not Disturb" sign up as the receptionist left the room.

"Hello everybody." The Detective began, "I'm sorry we're meeting for the first time under these circumstances. Please have a cup of coffee or a bite if you'd like, I'm sorry it's not more." Nobody was hungry or thirsty so the Detective continued, "Go ahead and have a seat around the table, this will not take long."

Katy walked over to Conrad and gave him a hug, then turned to Pedro and did the same. She then looked at Reina and asked, "Is this your wife?" Pedro confirmed and another embrace was necessary. Conrad walked around the table and greeted the family as they were about to sit. Handshakes and condolences were exchanged and everybody took a seat.

Detective Nelson took a seat at the head of the table, folded his hands in front of him, and looked up before addressing the loved ones. "As all of you now know, Cliff was murdered while he was working on

Tuesday morning." Tears were already pooling in Katy and Ms. Barry's eyes. "I can't begin to tell you how sorry I am, but I assure you I am going to do everything in my power to make sure that this is handled swiftly and properly. I knew Cliff, he was a sweetheart of a guy, and I'm crushed that something like this has happened in this neighborhood and in my territory. The next day or so is gonna be difficult, and decisions and arrangements need to be made and I regret that you have to go through this. I'm assuming you already know that we have the suspects in custody and a conviction should be fairly simple and swift. Conrad has a nice security system in The Tan Hat Man and the video was clear enough to show the perps and the events that unfolded."

Calvin interrupted, "Can we see the video?"

"I'm afraid not, at least not until the investigation is over and we have everything we need to get a conviction. I'm not sure you'd want to see it, it's rather graphic, but I assure you, having a brother myself, you would be very proud of Cliff. He defended himself with the fury of a Viking. It was only because he was outnumbered that he didn't prevail." Ms. Barry dropped her head and sobbed into a tissue that was at the ready. Calvin adjusted his seat and it was obvious that adrenaline was pumping through his veins. Sally noticed his jaw clinched and put her calming hand on his knee. Everyone else sat in silence. Detective Nelson continued, "I really just wanted to have this meeting to make everything official, meet all of you, and assure you we are doing the best we can. In doing so, if any of you have anything you think I should know, please feel free at this time to fill me in. If not, then I will send you on your way, as I know you have a lot to deal with. If this setting is uncomfortable, we can meet in private as well. The floor is open."

Ms. Barry looked up. "What kind of things are you talking about Detective?"

"Anything strange or out of the ordinary in your correspondence with him, or any behavior you may have felt out of character, especially those of you who see him on a regular basis. Conrad. Katy. Pedro.

Anything comes to mind that would give us some sort of reason or motive for this attack."

Everybody shook their heads slowly in agreement that nothing seemed out of the ordinary.

"I think the bastards were just trying to rob the bar." Conrad growled.

"Okay, well please feel free to call me if anything enters your mind. Anytime, day or night, any one of you. Thank you for meeting with me. I will leave you alone for a few minutes. I'll be just down the hall in my office. You are all free to leave. Conrad, please stop by the office on the way out." Detective Nelson rose from his chair and nodded in the direction of everyone before walking out of the room and closing the door behind him.

Everyone shifted in their chairs as Calvin stood up and stretched. Conrad took the initiative to start the conversation, "I'd like to invite all of you to dinner tonight. I have already made reservations at a little Italian restaurant where we can have a private table, and I'd be honored if you'd join me. I will understand if you decline."

Mr. Barry stood from his seat and said, "Yes of course we'll be there."

Everyone began to stand up and push in his or her chair, then turn toward the door. Mr. Barry than asked, to everyone, before the door was reached, "Did any of you notice anything strange going on with Cliff?" The communal reply came as a one big jumbled "No, not at all" to which he seemed relieved. "Okay good, I just wanted to be sure we were all on the same page. I don't want to be blind sided by something I didn't pick up on."

They opened the door and sifted out into to hall. Jumper held back and allowed everyone to get a head start before turning to Conrad, the last one in the room. "May I get in touch with you before we have dinner tonight sir?"

"Of course, is everything okay son?"

"Yes, I'd just like to have a few minutes of your time."

"Okay, well I have to meet with the Detective for a bit now. I should be done soon, how about meeting at noon?"

"Perfect." Jumper replied.

"There is a pizza shop right next to my bar. I'll meet you there."

"Sounds good." Jumper said and turned to see Mr. Barry waiting for him at the end of the hall. He stepped away from Conrad and headed towards the waiting Mr. Barry.

"What was that about?" Inquired Mr. Barry.

"Nothing really, I just have a question I wanna ask Cliff's boss. I'll tell you later."

"Everything alright?" Asked Mr. Barry.

"Yes, its fine."

As Conrad was entering the detective's office, Nelson stuck his head out and beckoned, "Mr. Barry?"

He let Jumper pass and walked back to the office.

Detective Nelson handed Mr. Barry a slip of paper. "This is the number to the morgue. You'll need to contact them and make arrangements to have Cliff transferred back to Montana. I'm assuming that's where you'll have the funeral."

"I think so," said Mr. Barry, "but we'll probably have some sort of service here first, as we know Cliff had a lot of people who cared about him here."

"I think that's very kind Mr. Barry. He was a good kid."

They shook hands and Detective Nelson closed the door leaving Mr. Barry in the hallway wondering what on earth he needed to discuss with Conrad in private. He turned to find his way out of the building.

CHAPTER ELEVEN

Detective Nelson pulled a chair around to the back of the desk so Conrad could sit next to him and study the monitor. He pecked away at a couple of buttons on the keyboard in front him and the monitor instantly showed a frozen picture of the exact moment when Jimmy and Rodney entered the bar. Nelson hit another key and the screen split up into four different pictures, all of the exact same moment. The one on the bottom left of the screen showed the people sitting at the bar upon entry.

Nelson asked, "Do you know these guys?"

"I think so, can you make it bigger?"

A click on the keyboard and the screen was back to one frame.

"Well, that's Billy right there." Conrad said pointing to the Italian with the little mustache. "And those two there are Brian and Chris. They live up the block. They're roommates."

Nelson hit a few more buttons, advancing the frames a few more seconds and switching the angle to one showing the big man exiting the restroom. "What about him?"

"You know him." Said Conrad. "That's Red! He's in there every night. He's the chef at Ca va Bien, stops in on his way home from work."

"Oh yeah, of course." Nelson said and then asked "Anything out of the ordinary with these clowns?"

"No. I have numbers for all of them. No way they have anything to do with it, but we can call them. I thought you said Pauly was on here."

"I think he is," Nelson said as he tapped a few keys bringing the screen to about 90 minutes prior.

He split the screen up four ways again and some different patrons were at the tables minding their own business. The pretty young lady was cut off, but it was clear that somebody was sitting just off camera as Cliff often addressed the spot with which she was sitting, delivered a drink, and handed her some sort of piece of paper that he retrieved several minutes later. The angle with the other patrons was then pulled up full screen again. "Is that Pauly?" asked Nelson.

"Sure as hell is," Snapped Conrad.

"He leaves here in couple minutes," Nelson said as he was punching more keys. "Cliff grabs that piece of paper that I think was exchanged with the girl, heads to the basement, Pauly slams his beer, throws money on the bar, pulls out his cell phone and appears to say goodbye as he sticks the phone to his ear." The screen was now playing everything Nelson just said. There were a few other people at the bar, but nothing seemed out of the ordinary. Conrad recognized them, but didn't know their names.

"I wanna get in touch with Red, Billy, Chris and Brian and find out what they know. I wanna know what was on the piece of paper, I wanna know who the girl was, and I wanna know why Pauly was in such a haste to finish up when Cliff disappeared. I think that bastard is acting awfully strange physically. I'm gonna call the others first, I'd appreciate if you didn't try to get in touch with Pauly until I talk to the others and get my questioning in this afternoon. Can you do that?"

"Of course," said Conrad, "If you'd like to call them from my phone, I'm guessing you'll have better luck getting an answer."

"Not a bad idea, why don't you call them now and just let them know to expect a call from me within the hour, and let them know I'm only asking if they saw or heard anything strange the night they were there."

"Billy actually tried to call me three times yesterday but I wasn't in the mood to talk. I assumed if he knew something, he'd call you. He never left a message. I'll call him first." Conrad stood up from his chair and moved it around to the other side of the desk. He settled back in and pulled out his phone and got to work. Detective Nelson pulled out a file and began looking over it while he waited for the okay to make his own calls.

~

Everyone from the meeting, sans Conrad and Detective Nelson, was standing in front of the police station on the sidewalk. They all exchanged cell phone numbers and made plans to meet at a pub down the block from the restaurant before the dinner that Conrad had planned. Katy gave everybody directions. Calvin, Sally and Mr. and Ms. Barry were going to go down to the NYU Medical Center to start the process of getting Cliff back to Montana. Pedro and Reina assured everyone they would be at dinner. Jumper opted to go to the park to kill some time. Katy wanted to join Jumper. The Barry's hailed a cab and the other four began walking west. Once they approached Lexington Avenue, Pedro and Reina turned north to get to the subway station. Katy and Jumper continued on to Central Park. Once alone,

Katy said to Jumper, "Listen, I have keys to Cliff's apartment. What should I do with them?"

Jumper thought for a moment, "Just hang on to them for now. We'll give them to the Barry's later and they can decide what to do."

"I know it sounds ridiculous, but I have some personal items that I'd like to get out of there before they all start rummaging through his things. Undergarments, feminine products, just some things I would like to keep sacred between Cliff and I if you know what I mean."

"Hmmm..." Jumper took another minute to ponder. "I have a meeting that I have to go to in two hours, why don't you go gather your things then. We'll get back together after the meeting. How does that sound?"

"A meeting? With who?" Katy asked.

"Don't worry about it, it's just something I need to do. I'll tell you about it when the time is right."

"Okay, that'll work. I only need to be there about five minutes. Thanks for understanding."

They continued to walk toward the park in silence as a nice breeze came around the nearing corner and brushed their faces.

"You know Cliff and I came to the park every day that we could. I think we were falling in love here." Katy suddenly welled up in tears again and Jumper put his arm around her. He was looking forward to the stories she would share over the next two hours.

~

The NYU Medical Center is a huge building with plenty of traffic coming in and out of it all day and night. The cab pulled up to the front and let the Barry family out. They walked through the doors that seemed to be the main entrance and found a small circular desk with a lady in official attire sitting in the middle. She'd clearly been there far too many years dealt with far too many impatient people. She was quick and short with them as they approached, barking, "Sign in please. Have your identification out."

She looked at each license and made sure the name and picture matched the face of the carrier then waved them towards a security guard by a metal detector. Ms. Barry politely began to ask, "Where might we find..." but was cut off by the lady in the circle desk. "See information, just past security."

They all looked up and saw the sign on the other side of the gate. With a shrug or two and the overwhelming circumstances, they emptied their pockets and walked through security. The information lady was a little less brash, but quick to inform as well. Mr. Barry decided it was his turn to deal with the New York City style of doing things. He approached and she looked up from her paperwork.

"Excuse me, our son was admitted here yesterday. We need to find him and talk to somebody."

"What is his name?" she asked as she pulled her monitor toward her and plucked on the keyboard.

"Clifford James Barry" replied Mr. Barry. The receptionist froze. She didn't need to punch any more buttons. She looked at them and said, "I'm so sorry," as she took a folder and put it strategically on top of her New York Post that was sitting amongst her paperwork. "You'll need to go down two levels to the morgue. When you get off of the elevator, the reception desk will be there to help you."

"Thank you," said Mr. Barry and the rest of them half heartedly nodded as they passed her, heading toward the elevator.

Arriving at level B2, the family slowly moved out and saw the desk directly in front of them. They walked up to the lady behind the counter who had a much softer demeanor about her than the ladies encountered on the main floor. Dealing with the families of lost ones takes a special kind of person. She politely asked, "What can I help you with?"

"We're the Barry family," Mr. Barry said, "I believe our son is here."

"Oh my, yes. I believe I spoke to you on the phone a bit ago. I have all of the paperwork pulled for you. I'm very sorry for your loss."

"Thank you."

She continued, "This will take a little while to fill out. Have a seat in the waiting area and I'll bring it to you. Did you bring all of your information? Identification?"

"Yes."

"And have you made a decision on what to do with his body?"

"Yes, we're having it transported to Montana for burial, but we plan to have a service in New York."

Calvin had heard enough and turned with Sally in tow to have a seat while his parents dealt with the logistics.

"Given the nature of the way in which the deceased lost his life, I'd recommend a closed casket ceremony. Of course that is up to you, but if you go that route, you may choose to have the service in New York without the casket. This way the body only needs to be moved once." Suggested the receptionist.

"Can we see the body?"

"Only immediate family," came the reply.

"We'd like to see him before we make that decision," confirmed Ms. Barry.

"I'll have somebody take you in. Have a seat for a few minutes. We'll deal with the paperwork when you return. How many will be going in?"

Mr. Barry opened his mouth to speak. He wasn't quite sure if Cliff's mother could handle seeing her oldest son's dead body. Hell, he wasn't sure if he could handle it. His thought process made no difference, however, because the answer came immediately.

"Three." Said Ms. Barry. "Mother, Father and Brother."

"Okay Ms. Barry, have your ID's out and I'll get you in as soon as I can."

They turned to have a seat and Mr. Barry commented only loud enough for Ms. Barry to hear, "How many times are we gonna have to show our Goddamned ID's?"

CHAPTER TWELVE

Billy answered the phone on the second ring. Conrad apologized for not picking up the phone yesterday. Billy understood, but explained that he called as soon as he heard the news because he was sure he could provide a solid description of the two strangers that entered the bar just before he left. After seeing the news footage in the afternoon, he let it be, assuming the photos were a much better help than any second-hand-at-a-glance description he was able to give. He only regretted that he didn't wait with Cliff until he closed, as he felt uneasy about the two characters in the bar at that hour. It was something he'll never forgive himself for. Conrad explained that the detective was going to be calling soon to gather any information about a possible motive or reason for the useless killing.

"Well hell," Billy jumped in. "You didn't hear?"

"Hear what?" Conrad immediately asked with concern.

"I guarantee they came in to get the lotto ticket."

"What lotto ticket?" Conrad asked with impatience.

"Cliff won something on some scratch off lotto ticket. He let some young girl scratch it off for him and she said he won a half million dollars. He ran downstairs and locked it up, said he'd get it the next day but wouldn't show anyone. That fuckin Pauly went running out of the bar right after. I guarantee he went runnin his mouth to somebody, which is how Cliff got cornered. I didn't put two and two together at the time cuz I was pretty drunk. I would have never left."

"Are you fuckin serious?" Conrad couldn't help but to curse in disbelief.

Detective Nelson was listening but getting antsy. He finally motioned for Conrad to hand over his phone, but Conrad put up his finger signaling just one more minute.

Conrad continued, "Did you say he put it in the office?"

"Fuckin right! Did they get it?"

"I don't think so. The office door was locked tight when we arrived."

"Well it's fuckin in there then."

"I'm gonna put you on with Nelson now. Just tell him what you told me."

"Okay," Billy was replying as the phone was being handed over.

"How ya doing Billy? Been a long time," said Detective Nelson.

Conrad sat back in his chair and ran his fingers through his hair as Billy rehashed his story to Detective Nelson. *The safe hadn't been opened in three days. Was there really a winning lottery ticket in there?*

~

The lady behind the desk in the morgue finally came around to the Barry's and asked them to follow her. Sally stood and kissed Calvin on the cheek, then sat back down. They walked them down a hall and finally to a door. She left them there and headed back to her post. They opened the door and found another sign-in sheet and another official that wanted to see identification. After they were all signed in and confirmed their identities, they followed the hospital employee down a row of doors that seemed like it was a mile long. When they finally arrived to what appeared to be the proper refrigerator, he stopped and turned to the family. "I feel it only necessary to warn you that he went through quite an ordeal before arriving here, and if you don't want to see it, you are more than welcome to change your mind." Calvin and Mr. Barry both looked at Ms. Barry, which seemed to irritate her. "No thanks," she replied, "I'm ready."

The door was slowly opened and the foot of Cliff was immediately visible with a tag dangling from a toe. It bared his name and some numbers, sure to coincide with some sort of labeling system and some coroner code. The table was then pulled out of the square shaped tube and the family stood in anticipation. After a moment, the morgue assistant stepped to the head of the body and pulled back the cover. Ms. Barry gasped, turned her head, and buried it into Mr. Barry, who simply put his massive arm around her while he stood there and looked at his son. He didn't move, just stared, and a tear rolled down the inside of his cheek until it finally made its way to the end of his nose. Calvin seemed to double in size; he puffed up with all the anger, air, and testosterone any one man can have. He turned and headed for the door, looking like the Incredible Hulk as he walked toward the exit.

Another moment passed and Mr. Barry nodded that he'd seen enough. He turned with Ms. Barry under his arm and walked toward the exit as the sound of the table being pushed back in and the door being sealed shut echoed through the hallway. They opened the door and stepped back out into the hallway to return to the waiting area. Calvin was pacing just to the right of the door he'd just exited. His nose was red and eyes were bloodshot. He was fighting back tears and exhaling heavily as if he was just about to enter the ring for a title fight. He hopped around and kept pacing, making no sound but the heavy breath. Tears were streaming. He was about to explode.

Mr. Barry leaned in to Ms. Barry's ear and said, "Go on down and sit with Sally, we'll be there in a second." Ms. Barry did as she was told and Calvin's father turned to him.

"Come here son."

"Dad! I can't handle this Dad! I'm gonna lose it. I can't handle this."

The pacing never stopped, the breathing was heavy and the voice was broken yet stern, and much louder than he intended. Mr. Barry opened his arms and stepped into his son.

"Daaaaad. I can't take this."

"I know bud, keep it together. Your mother needs you to keep it together."

"I don't know that I can Dad! I don't know that I can."

And with that, Mr. Barry embraced his youngest son. He squeezed tight and Calvin returned the squeeze in defeat. He let lose all of the emotions any brother could have for another and buried his face into his Dad's shirt. They stood there and hugged, and cried, and rocked and swayed and cried and wept. Calvin was having trouble breathing but only squeezed harder. Snot and drool and tears and mucus were coming out of his face and soaking his father's shirt as he wailed, and his father was now crying along with him. They stood there and hugged and cried some more, until it had finally run its course. Calvin then loosened up, triggering the release from his father, in turn allowing Calvin to release. He ran his hand over his face, used his forearm to swipe his nose, then looked at his Dad's shirt and began to laugh. Nothing was funny, but laughter often seems to come after an embarrassing meltdown. Mr. Barry took his son's jaw in both hands, looked him straight in the eye, and said, "C'mon son." They turned and walked down the hall towards the waiting area where Ms. Barry sat with her head buried in Sally's shoulder.

~

Jumper had enjoyed the fresh air of Central Park and the stories that Katy had shared about all the fun times she'd had with Cliff in the park. Playing catch with a baseball or throwing a football, tossing a Frisbee or having a picnic, drinking wine and watching the Philharmonic. They'd seen a few plays during summer stage, had drinks at the Boathouse, rented a rowboat for an hour one afternoon and often stopped to watch the goofy roller skaters dancing around like it was 1984. All of the exercising, jogging, racing, wrestling around, and the inevitable kiss that seemed to complete every story she shared were all exactly how Jumper imagined Cliff would treat his current girlfriend. That's the kind of guy he was. Always up for an adventure, always excited to be a part of whatever was happening at the moment, and always glad to share his good times with someone he cared about. It was an hour and half of amazing conversation, and he was glad he got to hear every word of it.

It was just past 11:30, time for Jumper and Katy to head back toward the east side so that he could have his meeting with Conrad. They walked past Lexington Avenue and Katy gave Jumper directions to get to the pizzeria that he was supposed to go to. He gave her a quick hug and assured her he'd call as soon as his meeting was over, but before he let her go, he looked at her and got serious for a moment.

"I don't think I need to say this, you've given me no reason not to trust you, so please don't give me one today. Just go to Cliff's get your stuff and leave the apartment. Are we good on that?"

"Of course." She replied but was uncomfortable with the exchange. It seemed to come out of left field and her expression made her surprise obvious to Jumper. He instantly felt guilty, probably came on too strong, but he was doing it for the sake of Cliff's wishes.

"I'll see you in an hour or so." He again confirmed as Katy turned and walked away.

CHAPTER THIRTEEN

The paperwork seemed to take forever. They decided to forego a service in New York all together, figuring without the casket and not knowing anybody other than who they'd met this morning, they could save a full round of condolences from complete strangers. They knew what a wonderful person he was. They knew people loved him. They knew wakes were an inconvenience for everyone. The decided to simply ship him back home and plan for the full service there. They decided they would offer to spend the money saved on the service in New York to fly

Conrad, Pedro and Reina, and whatever travel cost Katy incurred out to Montana. Calvin was fine with the decision; he wanted to get out of this disgusting city as soon as possible.

~

Katy walked into the building with an eerie feeling. She was there just a couple of days ago. She didn't want to be there now. She felt intrusive. There had been so many magical evenings and sweaty mornings here. So many return trips from the gym or the park. So many glasses of wine. So many hugs and kisses. So many conversations. It had always been a safe and happy place. Now it seemed like a dungeon.

She put the key in the lock and turned it slowly. The smell was the same. The organized clutter was in place and the window was open as always. She went straight for the bottom drawer of the little dresser and opened it. Realizing she had nothing to carry her things in, she grabbed an empty CVS bag from a pile of empty bags in the kitchen. She returned to the drawer and began plucking her things out. She had two silk nighties and a couple pairs of panties with matching bras in the drawer. Beneath them was a red bustier complete with a garter belt and stockings that he'd given her for Valentines Day. She stuffed it all in the bag and then went to the bed. She pulled out a tiny shoebox that had some pictures of her in her red lingerie as well as a tiny vibrating sex toy they played with from time to time. She put it all in the bag and stood up. She looked around the room, paused and choked up before walking out of the apartment and locking the door safely behind her. It seemed so trivial, but she felt these were private affairs between the two them and wanted to keep them that way. She went to her apartment and buried the bag in her closet, sat on her bed, and waited to hear from Jumper.

~

The pizzeria had been there for years. The tables were old and the pictures on the wall were older. The massive ovens had clearly cooked tens of thousands of pizzas. Two buzzing little Hispanic men were busy behind the glass counter that displayed the pies with an array of toppings ready to be thrown in the heat and warmed up for anyone so inclined. Jumper stepped to the counter and ordered a bottle of lemonade. He paid $1.50 and turned to sit down just as Conrad entered the shop. Jumper set his drink down and thrust his hand toward Conrad.

"Thank you for meeting with me."

"Of course." He replied just as one of the men behind the counter shouted a hello to the old man. He nodded and threw a quick wave as he and Jumper sat at one of the rickety tables. "What can I do for you?"

"Well, I received a voicemail from Cliff the other night. Based on the time it came in and nature of the call, I think it was the last thing he did just before he died."

Conrad just looked quietly as Jumper went on.

"I haven't told anyone about the voicemail because it is of a rather personal nature."

"Did… or does, rather, he need something from me?"

"Well sort of, but I'm not sure it is something you have access too given the conversation that took place at the police station." A moment passed. "I need to know if you have a copy of the surveillance video from the murder."

Conrad didn't flinch. He looked at Jumper with intensity and after a moment he replied, "Why do you need to know that?"

"Well, I'll tell you what. I need your word that this stays between us."

"That what stays between us?" asked Conrad.

"I'd like to play the voicemail for you but I need to deliver its contents with care so I'd like you to allow me to do that, out of respect for Cliff."

"Of course."

"There is no reason for you to hear it if you don't have a copy of the tapes though. And that information will stay between us as well."

"I have a copy," replied Conrad.

Jumper pulled out his cell phone, punched a couple of keys, and handed the phone to Conrad. He took it from Jumper and held it to his ear. After the message was heard, he handed the phone back to Jumper and said, "Come with me son."

CHAPTER FOURTEEN

It was about half past noon when the Barry's were finally able to get out of the hospital. They agreed a light lunch was in order and figured they'd just get something close to the hotel so they could go for a nap and freshen up before going to dinner with Conrad. Calvin called Jumper to fill him in, but his phone went to voicemail. He didn't leave a message but sent a text message instead letting him know the plan. Sally called Katy at the same time, and invited her to lunch. She accepted the invitation and they decided to meet at T.G.I. Fridays on 42nd Street between Park and Madison Avenues, right around the corner from their hotel.

~

Detective Nelson entered the interrogation room where Jimmy sat on the other side of a small square table. Nelson sat on the other side of the table, punched record on the sound device, and confirmed that he'd been read his Miranda rights. Jimmy sat still and didn't seem nervous at all. He was never scared of cops, but he definitely didn't enjoy their company. After a short pause, Detective Nelson asked, "Would you like to tell me why you killed Clifford Barry?"

"I'll tell you anything you want, but you gotta let Rodney go. He didn't have anything to do with it."

"Rodney has been charged with a lesser crime, but he cannot simply be set free given his assistance in the crime."

"He didn't do nothin."

"We have the surveillance video Jimmy, and maybe you don't remember or didn't see it, but he hit

Mr. Barry with a pool stick in the head, allowing you to gain the upper hand in the fight."

"He was just protecting me," Rodney seemed defeated already.

"And therein lies the problem. Assisting you with a criminal activity is also a crime."

"What is he lookin at?"

"He'll do some time without question, but it will not be close to what you're going to do."

"So why should I tell you anything then?"

Detective Nelson shifted his seat and carefully chose his words. "You are looking at life in prison. Based on the evidence we have with the video alone, that's what you'll get. If there were other parties involved, or any reason we should know that caused you to act this way, we may be able to get you paroled someday. I'd like to know how you heard about the lotto ticket."

"What makes you think I was there about the lotto ticket?"

"Well for one, you basically just admitted that there even was a lotto ticket. If there wasn't, you may have asked 'What lotto ticket' but since you didn't, I assume you knew about it."

"Okay, so. I was there for the lotto ticket. I'd heard about it, heard it was a lot of money, so I went to get it."

"How did you hear about it?" asked Detective Nelson.

"It just came to me through the grapevine," smirked Jimmy.

"You know Jimmy, I will have your cell phone records by the end of the day, and I will know every call that was made that evening. If you received a call, you may as well tell me who it was and save us both a lot of time."

Jimmy just sat and stared at the table. He wasn't sure if it would matter to give up Pauly. He wasn't sure how Pauly had heard about the ticket. *Was he in the bar that night?*

"I get a lot of calls," Jimmy finally said.

"I'm sure you do. But if any of the numbers on your phone record match any of the numbers of one of the few men that were in that bar that night, we'll be bringing them in. We have a list of everybody that was a patron that night and video of all of them."

"I got the info from a call, but I don't know where it came from."

"The name Pauly wouldn't ring a bell would it?"

"Yes."

"Okay. That's about all I need to know from you Jimmy. I just want to know one more thing. Once he was out of commission, why did you have to crush his face with the barstool? The final blow seems to be what killed him. Seems so unnecessary."

"I didn't want to kill the dude, it just happened."

"All for a lotto ticket that you didn't even get."

Detective Nelson walked out of the room and behind the glass where another detective was waiting. They watched as a guard took Jimmy out of the room and a few minutes later Rodney was brought in. He was clearly scared. He was practically shivering when they put him in his chair. Detective Nelson let him sit there for five minutes before entering the room and going over the same initial procedures.

"Why don't you tell me what happened."

Rodney's voice was shaking. "I don't really know. I was just with Jimmy and we went to a bar, I went to the bathroom, and when I came out, they were fighting."

"So you didn't know why they were fighting?"

"Jimmy told me he had something to pick up. That's all I knew."

"Why did you hit the victim with a pool cue?"

"I was hoping it would be enough to knock him out so that we could leave, but it wasn't. I'm too small for those guys."

"What was Jimmy going to collect?"

"I don't know. We were hangin' on the block, he got a phone call from this guy Pauly that he knows and said he had to do a favor for him. I didn't really think about it, Jimmy is my friend so I went along for the ride. I had no idea what we were going to do."

Detective Nelson didn't need much more information from Rodney. Neither he nor Rodney was going to be released so if he had more questions, he could talk to him later. His case was pretty much solved. He'd hand over all the evidence and let the courts do their thing. Technology has made fighting crime so much easier.

~

Conrad walked passed the entrance to The Tan Hat Man with Jumper at his side. The bar was still closed. He wasn't sure when or even if he'd open it again. He didn't really care at the moment. They walked around to the side entrance leading to the basement and Conrad pulled out his keys. After a few locks and doors, Jumper was in the office with Conrad. He fired up the computer and clicked a couple of files. He'd watched the video more than twenty times after the detectives left. Sometimes he was proud of Cliff and his valiant effort, but mostly he was just angry and confused. He wished there was sound to see what was said leading up to the battle, but he had watched it so many times that he had a version that was pretty close to the way it happened.

Once he had the file pulled up, he turned and looked at Jumper. "I need your word that you will not watch this. I'm gonna burn you a copy and you give it directly to his father, is that understood? The directions in your voicemail are very clear, and since he trusted you to deliver his wishes, I'll trust you with this copy. Tell me that I can do that."

"Absolutely sir." Jumper said. "Truthfully, I have a weak stomach and I don't think I could see it. I don't even like cage fighting on TV, much less my best friend in the fight for his life. I would have been a shitty soldier."

This satisfied Conrad. He grabbed a blank disc from a spindle on a shelf and stuck in the computer, hit a few keys and the copy was in progress.

"How do you plan to handle the others?" Conrad asked while they waited.

"I haven't figured that out yet, I'll probably ask Mr. Barry for advice on that one."

"That's probably wise," Conrad agreed as the disc popped out. "Guard that with your life. I'll see you at dinner."

Jumper put the disc in his back pocket and walked out of the office. Conrad turned in his chair, spun the lock and opened the safe. There it was, leisurely thrown on top of stacks of singles, the lotto ticket. Conrad picked it up, looked at it carefully and shook his head, mumbling, "a half a million dollars."

CHAPTER FIFTEEN

Detective Nelson was in his car on the way back to his office when his phone rang. The caller id displayed "Conrad Bar" so he hit the command to answer.

"Whats up?"

"Billy was right. There is a lotto ticket worth a half a million dollars sitting in my safe."

"Okay. Stay put. I'll be by in about 10 minutes to collect that as evidence."

"Wait a minute, this should go to his family," Conrad snapped.

"Relax Conrad. It will. Nobody will get their paws on it. There is no dispute as to whom the ticket belongs to so I'll make sure the proper channels are taken to get the money to his parents."

"Don't fuck these people Nelson, they're going through enough."

"I'll see you in a minute," replied Nelson as he terminated the call and headed to The Tan Hat Man.

~

Jumper walked into T.G.I. Fridays and looked around until he saw Katy and the Barry's sitting at a table. He walked up and took the empty chair that was waiting for him. It was quiet and everybody seemed exhausted. The waitress showed up and Jumper ordered a small salad with a Cranberry Juice as the others were picking at whatever they had ordered. His food arrived almost immediately and they all finished in silence, paid the check, and decided it was time for a nap.

~

Detective Nelson picked up the lotto ticket at The Tan Hat Man. Conrad insisted he go along until the ticket was officially admitted as evidence. This irritated Nelson, giving he was law enforcement and a friend of Conrad, but given the number of dirty cops and high end white collar crime that has been ever rising in the city and the country, he understood and allowed him to come along. Once that was over, Conrad jumped in a cab to get some rest before dinner while Detective Nelson returned to his office.

The warrant had been issued for the arrest of Pauly and Nelson was just waiting for the phone call to know his boys in blue had completed their assignment. Pauly was already on probation for taking sports bets and a couple other petty crimes, and Nelson hoped he could get the felony conspiracy charge to stick on this one to get him locked away for a long time. The cell phone records were easy, the video from the bar placed him there, and the testimony of Rodney and especially Jimmy should be enough. He could only hope. Crooks like this always seemed to have a way of sneaking through the system because they never actually get caught with their hand in the cookie jar.

~

Katy hugged everybody outside Friday's and jumped in a cab to rest up before the dinner in the evening. The Barry family walked around the corner and entered their hotel. Everybody was asleep almost immediately.

CHAPTER SIXTEEN

The restaurant was called "Nicky's Italiano." It was a quaint little family owned place located on the corner of 77th St. and 2nd Avenue in Manhattan. It only held about 100 customers when it was full. It had two rooms packed with tables. The main dining area held the majority of the tables and the back room held the rest. It was often used for private parties and wasn't seated until the front of the house was full. Many small rehearsal dinners, birthday parties, and graduation celebrations were held there. It could only hold 26 people.

Nicky was a longtime friend of Conrad and had no problem making sure that the private room was his for the evening. He and his guests would be treated like royalty, and Conrad knew that Nicky and his staff knew how to make that happen. He'd stopped in earlier in the day and put his American Express card on file, asked that a 22% gratuity be added for the staff, and made certain that a bill or even talk of a bill didn't come to the room. He chose a nice dry Cabernet and a pleasant Pinot Grigio and was assured that nobody would have an empty glass for the entire evening. If somebody preferred beer or a cocktail, that was okay as well. He arranged to stop in the tomorrow to pick up the final tally and a receipt. Trust was not an issue with these old friends.

~

Detective Nelson was waiting when Pauly walked through the door. They exchanged nods as Pauly went to get his photo snapped and fingerprints taken. He was immediately transferred to an interrogation room for Nelson to ask some questions. He entered the room with disappointment.

"What did you do Pauly, huh?"

"I don't know what you're talking about."

"Jimmy told me you called and threatened him, said he had to go get a lotto ticket for you. And I'll have the cell phone records to see precisely when and what calls were made. I also have you on video about an hour and a half before those two idiots you called come into the bar. You can tell me about it or not, either way, I've got enough to send you away for a long time Pauly."

"So what the fuck am I doing here?" snapped Pauly. "You offering me a deal or something?"

"No deal. Not this time. I just wanted to see if you had a statement or a story that you'd like to go on record."

Pauly leaned forward. "Go fuck yourself Nelson."

The Detective stood and locked eyes with Pauly for a moment then turned and left the room.

~

Jumper shot Katy a text message. "Can you bring Cliff's keys to dinner please?" She was just getting out of the shower and had a towel wrapped around her head. She picked up her phone and replied, "No problem." She didn't care at this point, she went and had a copy made after she'd collected her things anyway. She didn't really have a reason, in case she forgot something maybe, but they would probably never get used.

~

The main room at "Nicky's Italiano" was about half full when Conrad arrived. He was about fifteen minutes early, but was already later than Katy, Pedro and Reina who were sitting at the tiny bar, a glass of wine in front of each of them. Nicky rushed to greet Conrad and take him into the private room as the three at the bar collected their things. They walked into the private room that had the tables in a line and set beautifully for ten complete with a glass of ice water in front of every setting. Frank Sinatra was singing softly in the background. Candles were lit around the room and on the tables. There were baskets of bread with ramekins of butter next to each.

Nicky perked up, obviously hearing something that didn't register with the rest of them, and disappeared into the main room. Pedro and Reina sat on one side at the far end of the table and Conrad and Katy assumed the seats directly across from them. Just as they were about to actually sit down, Nicky appeared again showing Jumper and the Barry family to the dining room. Ms. Barry moved in next to Katy, followed by Sally and Calvin. Jumper went to the other side, took the seat next to Reina and Mr. Barry sat next to him. The tenth seat stayed unoccupied. Nicky quickly asked what everybody would like to drink. The men and Katy chose red wine, the women white, but Mr. Barry was going to have a Heineken. (They didn't carry Budweiser at Nicky's) Nicky disappeared and two waiters took his place. They set a few appetizers around the table, explained what they were, and disappeared again. The wine was delivered promptly and it was time to pray.

~

After the "Amen," the glasses were raised and a "cheers" was in order celebrating the loving prayer and the amazing dinner they were about to devour. Everybody began picking at the appetizers and passing them around until the waiters came in with options for salads and dinners. They didn't have a menu; Nicky chose his best two salads and a soup, and his 5 best entrees. They were delivered vocally from a waiter and when the decisions were made, they were mentally clocked in the waiter's brain. Mr. Barry looked a bit bewildered; he'd never seen a waiter or waitress not write down an order, ever!

Conversation started to flourish as the appetizers were disappearing and the wine was entering the bloodstreams. The appetizer dishes were cleared and nine salads were delivered. There were lots of moans and groans insinuating the deliciousness of the affair, and the mood was lightening. There were even a couple laughs and giggles starting to fill the room. The entrée's arrived and the feast continued. There was salmon and steak and pasta and duck with every imaginable side dish scattered about the table. The wine was moving and the plates were emptying quickly. The mood was relatively festive, and it seemed that everyone in the room had in the back of their minds that this is what Cliff would want. The final bites were being consumed and the waiters and a busboy were clearing the table. Conrad stood up as everybody was finishing and sipping on wine and water.

"I'd like to say a few words, if you don't mind."

Everyone got quiet, set down their glasses and turned their attention to Conrad.

"I'd like to thank you all very much for having dinner with me. It is an honor to meet the people behind the scenes of one of the best young men I've ever had the pleasure of befriending and working with. This neighborhood, my bar, and everyone around are better off for having known Cliff, and I am honored to call him a friend. If you don't mind, I'd like to tell you one of my favorite stories."

Everyone around the table settled in and was excited to hear what Conrad had to say.

"Cliff had only been working with me for about five months. It was snowy evening and the Super, his name is Sid, from the building across the street from my place, came in and took a stool at the end of the bar next to me. Cliff approached with his usual smile asked what Sid would like. Sid, without ordering and clearly in a foul mood, asked Cliff, 'What are you so happy about?' Cliff simply replied, 'We're alive. We're in good health. What more do we need?' Sid snapped back, 'Life is shit. This weather sucks. Ain't nothin to be happy about.' Cliff stood there a moment, then looked at grouchy old Sid and said, 'You're always in a bad mood. Why in the world are you so bitter?' Sid replied, 'I've worked my whole life and I have nothing to show for it kid.' 'Is that what you think life is about, having something to show?' Cliff asked. So Sid was quiet for a minute while he peeled off his hat and coat and Cliff went to get a drink for another patron. When he returned, Sid said, 'Just watching you smile all the time is tiring.' Cliff said, 'I'm happy Sid. It's easier than you think.' 'How's that?' asked Sid. 'Do you have the secret to happiness that you'd like to share with me?' Cliff kind of laughed and smiled. Then he looked at him very seriously and said, 'Actually, I think I do. Do you really think a young pup like me can teach something to an old dog like you?' Sid laughed and shook his head, 'I doubt it, but this oughtta be good.' So Cliff squared off behind the bar, bent over to get level with Sid, and said to him, 'Well, I could die right now without one single regret because everybody I love, knows I love them. There is not one important person in my life that doesn't know how important they are to me, and that, my man, lets me sleep well at night. That's my secret Sid, love the ones you love and don't let them doubt it. When its all over, you've left the world with something no money can buy.'"

Ms. Barry pulled her napkin from her lap and was dabbing away tears. The rest of the table sat motionless and let the story soak in. Calvin exhaled heavily but refused to shed a tear at this dinner. Nicky had entered the room during the story and stood in the doorway. Both Katy and Sally were looking up in attempt to avoid any moisture leaving their eyes.

Conrad let them sit for a moment before raising his glass, "To Cliff." The sounds of glasses clattering filled the room and everyone took a drink. Then he said, "I have some good news for you. It's good on two levels. The first, we have figured out why these thugs came after Cliff. I was relieved to hear that he was not involved or mixed up in something underground or illegal, even though that thought had never really crossed my mind. The truth is Cliff had picked up a scratch off lottery ticket on the way to work that night. When he and a friend scratched it off, they found that he'd won five hundred thousand dollars. One of the guys at the bar ran his mouth off when he left, the information got into the wrong hands, and just before he was going close up for the night, they came in to rob him of the ticket. I don't why Cliff didn't just give them the ticket, maybe he figured he was going to be harmed either way, but the thugs never got the ticket. Cliff had locked it in the safe long before they had arrived. I found it this morning, called Detective Nelson, and he assured me that the ticket would be given to the family. I went to the precinct with him to be sure that it was properly admitted as evidence as I don't trust too many people these days. He said he's going to call the judge tomorrow to find out when you can claim his prize."

Ms. Barry lost it. "He died over a LOTTO TICKET!" she screamed.

Calvin jumped up and hopped behind his mother, bending over and bear-hugging her. "Mom, he would have given it to them if he'd had a choice. You know Cliff is smarter than that. He had to feel he was in trouble Mom, it's the only thing that makes sense." She buried her face in Calvin's elbow and cried for a moment while the rest of the table sat silent. After a moment, she looked up and said, "Okay everybody, I'm fine. I swear. I'm fine. I apologize for the outburst. Calvin is correct; I have to trust Clifford's judgment." The table relaxed a bit. Conrad sat down as Calvin returned to his seat.

The waiters returned with offers of coffee, after dinner drinks, and several small plates with forks and spoons were placed in front of everybody. They showed up with four glorious desserts and they were passed around the table. Everybody was so full that they were only taking a bite or two from each dish for their plate. Coffees and cappuccino's arrived and the table started to talk again, but now the conversation was geared toward the fact that Cliff had won the lottery. A couple jokes were cracked and some small laughs were shared. Cliff won the lottery. It figured.

~

After all of the dessert plates were cleared and everybody had clearly had their fill, it seemed time to wrap up the dinner. Calvin stood up and looked toward the opposite end of the table. "I just want to apologize for being so quiet since I've been here. I want you all to know how much my family and I appreciate everything you've done for Cliff. He always spoke very highly of his friends and co-workers since he's moved out here, and you should know that we are really grateful that you all made him feel welcome." He sat back down. Conrad sat still; Katy looked down at the table, as did Reina. Pedro squirmed a bit and then stood up.

"I would like to say something. Please forgib my English. Most people don't know how much I lub Cleef. He was a bery good friend. He come to all of my daughter birthday party, he come play football with my family, and he help me make a bideo slide show for my wife for Balentine Day. He was planning to come with us to bisit my family in Mexico next year. He is bery famous there, I tell them all about him. I will miss him. May he rest in peace."

Ms. Barry couldn't help it. She started crying again. Calvin got up and walked around the table. He gave Pedro a big hug and some solid pats on the back. The rest of the table began to stand up, stretch a bit, and pass out some hugs. Everybody addressed Conrad individually, thanked him for dinner, and gave him a hug. Reina stood by Pedro the whole time.

When Ms. Barry came to hug Pedro and Reina, Reina took Ms. Barry's hands and said, "Cliff meant a lot to my husband and our daughter. She was always very excited when she knew he was joining our family. He always brought her a gift. Her favorite is a movie he gave her called 'Pete's Dragon.' He said it was his favorite movie when he was a child." Ms. Barry began to cry yet again and gave Reina a massive hug.

~

Katy offered to take everybody to a little pub around up the block for a drink. They all went and ordered an array of nightcaps. As they all received their drinks and headed off to get situated around a table in the corner, Jumper waited by the bar while Katy paid for the round. When everybody was out of earshot, he said, "I need a couple minutes alone with you."

"I have the keys for you." She replied.

"No, its not that, it's a message from Cliff."

"What are you talking about?" Katy asked a little irritated.

"I'll explain after everyone leaves. Just hang back when the family calls it a night and we'll have a chat."

"Alright." She said. "I'm not gonna be able to sleep anyway."

CHAPTER SEVENTEEN

Conrad assured the Barry family that he would call them tomorrow if he heard anything new and told them he'd be at the funeral in Montana. They thanked him again and piled into a cab to head back to the hotel. They were full and exhausted. Jumper told them he'd be there in a bit, was going to stay and have one more drink with Katy and Conrad. Calvin wanted to hang back as well, but decided any more drinks could stir him to a place he didn't need to go. Pedro and Reina said goodbye as well, they had to pick up their daughter from the babysitter.

After the bar was cleared of the family, Jumper got a round of drinks from the bar and brought it to the table where Conrad and Katy waited. She was tired as well so she wasted no time, "What did you wanna talk to me about?"

Jumper pulled out his cell phone and set it on the table. Conrad sat quietly and waited to see how Jumper would handle the situation.

"I received a phone call from Cliff. I think it was right before he died. It's a little tough to understand, I believe it was after the fight. He left a message and I want you to hear it."

Katy shifted and said, "Why are you just now bringing this up?"

"When you listen to the message, you'll see why. After you hear it, we'll need to go over to his apartment."

"Okay, well I'm done. Let's go. I wanna hear the message."

The three of them took a long pull from each of their full drinks, left them half full on the table, got up and walked out of the bar to the curb. Jumper punched a couple buttons on the phone and handed it to Katy. She listened intently, and her face went white. After she'd heard it, she handed the phone to Jumper and fought back emotion. She looked at Conrad and asked, "You've heard this?"

"Yes."

"Who else?"

Jumper replied, "Nobody, I'll handle the rest tomorrow. He wanted me to get a book out of his apartment, and I wanted to do it before it became mayhem. He asked for me specifically to get it, so I wanted to do that with as little conflict or interference as possible. Do you know where the book is?"

"I have no idea, but we'll find it. It can't be too hard, there isn't much in there."

"Okay, let's get a cab."

"I'd like you to come with us Conrad." Katy said.

"I wouldn't have it any other way sweetheart."

~

The cab pulled up to the building that Katy was in earlier in the day to get her personal belongings. Conrad and Katy stepped out while Jumper paid the driver. Once all three were on the street, Jumper looked up and saw the open window. He sort of laughed, thinking of all the times he'd complained about it being too hot or too cold but Cliff never budged. He had to have his fresh air.

Katy dug in her purse and pulled out the set of keys. She opened the front door and then the second door as Conrad and Jumper walked into the building. They walked up the stairs and arrived at Cliff's door. She put the key in and turned it, opened the door and hit the light switch. Just before the door was closed, the neighbor opened his door and stuck his head out. Only seeing Jumper and Conrad, he quickly clipped, "Who the hell are you guys?" Katy stuck her head back out of the door, which seemed to let the neighbor relax.

"Hey Patrick," she said.

"Oh hell Katy, I was about to call the cops! I didn't think anybody would be here until Cliff's family got here. I'm really sorry about Cliff by the way, he was the best neighbor ever."

"Yeah, it's been a rough day. Don't call the cops, this is his best friend Jumper and..."

"Oh hell Conrad!" Pat replied finally recognizing him from the bar. "Sorry about that, I'm not used to seeing you outside of the 'Hat Man.'"

"Don't worry about it son, I'm glad to see he's got people looking after him."

"What are you guys looking for?" asked Pat.

Katy thought quick and made up a story about how she'd left a bag, her calendar, her camera and a book that she needed there but didn't want to come over all alone at this hour. Pat seemed appeased and went back into his apartment. Conrad, Jumper, and Katy closed the door and began their search.

~

Cliff was always sure that he was going to die young. He didn't know why or how, it was just a feeling he'd had since he was a very young boy. He took good care of his health and stayed away from trouble as often as he could. He assumed it would be something silly like a snowboarding accident or some freak occurrence like trying to save somebody from a tidal wave on a beach somewhere or something.

Since he'd always had this premonition, he always had everything prepared and mapped out in case he was correct. He didn't live in fear of it, which is probably why he was so calm when the day finally came. He'd decided long ago that he was going to make sure he didn't leave any loose ends to tie up, any apologies left unsaid, or any relationship damaged to the best of his ability. He couldn't live with the idea of having his last thoughts be those of regret.

He and Katy had a conversation one night involving religion and heaven and hell. Cliff explained his thoughts on the subject and was worried she'd be skeptical at the simplicity of it, especially since she and her family was Catholic. He definitely didn't want to offend her.

He didn't really believe in religion. He wasn't an atheist, but an agnostic. He accepted that there was a possibility, even the probability of a higher power, but did not subscribe to any organized religion. To him, it was all big business. He never forced his beliefs on anybody and didn't hold any disrespect for the many differing views and opinions that were out there. The fact is they are beliefs. He didn't even tell anyone in his family except Calvin where he stood on the subject because he didn't want to upset his parents or grandparents.

He simply felt that, in the last moment, before one dies, when the body and brain are shutting down, the thoughts that enter are the difference between heaven and hell. If you live with regret, and wish you'd told somebody you loved them but didn't, or apologize to someone and never got around to it, or done wrong by somebody and never attempted to make it right, well, simply put, that was hell. BUT, if you are at peace with your life, with the relationships you've created and nourished, if you've done everything in your power to do right when something has clearly gone wrong, then that is heaven. He only hoped and, for lack of a better word, prayed that his mind was in a place of serenity when that day arrived.

~

"I've listened to it a thousand times. The very last thing he said was, 'there is an old Montana phone book in my apartment that I need you to get and…' then it went blank," Jumper said. The three of them stood in the middle of the room and looked around for a minute. Katy made the first move, getting on her knees and looking underneath the bed. She pulled out a couple of shoeboxes and a plastic bin that when opened, just contained his snow clothes. She stood up and put her finger in her mouth while looking around for more options. Jumper was looking through some stock market books that were stacked next to his television. Nothing resembling the phone book. Conrad was on his toes looking on top of the cupboard above the kitchen sink. Katy and Jumper dug through the closets. Nothing. They all met in the center again, deep in thought. Conrad arched his back for a stretch then sat on the edge of the bed. Jumper moved the Papasan chair and made sure it wasn't hiding under the base of it. He stood after coming up empty. They looked around in defeat until suddenly Conrad pointed his finger at the wastebasket next to the computer.

"What the hell is that?" he asked.

Katy snatched the small wastebasket up and on the floor beneath it was the Missoula phone book. It was at least ten years old, dog eared and dirty. Nobody touched it. They simply stared at it for what seemed like forever.

CHAPTER EIGHTEEN

Jumper picked up the book and sat in Cliff's desk chair facing Katy and Conrad, where both were now sitting on the bed. The phone book was sitting in his lap. He put his hands on top of it and looked at the other two before saying, "I have no idea what we're going to find in here, but whatever it is, we're going to respect it. Are we all in agreement?" Neither vocalized a reply, but both nodded in agreement with certainty.

After another moment, Jumper peeled back the cover of the phone book. There was nothing different;

it just appeared to be an old phone book. He flipped through a page at a time looking for something, anything that would lead him in the right direction. After a few pages, he took his thumb and grabbed the bottom of the book and fanned the pages. They seemed to fan normally until he got about a third of the way into the book, when they seemed to be more flimsy. He stopped and peeled back the pages at about the halfway point of the book. Katy gasped.

~

The center of the book was completely hollowed out. It was an almost perfect rectangle that had been cut out with a razor blade. Sitting in the makeshift compartment were three things, two envelopes and a DVD. Jumper picked up the envelope on top. It was addressed to Cliff with a return address also bearing Cliffs address. It was post marked Jan. 2nd. In the bottom left-hand corner, highlighted with an orange highlighter pen, was Cliff scribbled handwriting. It said "Last Will and Testament! To be opened by my parents and my brother only." Jumper set it aside. Nobody had said a word yet. The second envelope was not sealed. When Jumper pulled back the flap, he was stunned to find it stuffed with $100.00 bills, fifty of them to be exact. He set that aside and pulled out the DVD. It was in a sleeve with a handwritten note. When jumper pulled out the note, it revealed the disc had been labeled "If I die." Jumper unfolded the handwritten note. It said, "Play this DVD at my funeral. Do NOT watch it beforehand. I appreciate it."

Jumper put the DVD and the note back in the sleeve just the way he found it. He then put all three items back in the phonebook and closed it. He looked at Conrad and Katy and said, "I think we should just leave this here and bring the Barry's here tomorrow."

Conrad said, "I'm a little worried about leaving that kind of cash in a vacant apartment."

"It'll be fine," Katy responded. "It's obviously been there for a long time and I don't think anybody but us knows about it."

"It's up to you two, but if we do that, I think we should close and lock that window," Conrad returned.

"Good idea," Jumper said before moving to return the book to its original resting place underneath the wastebasket. Conrad got up and handled the window. Katy was staring at the floor.

"Everybody better get some sleep." Conrad said after securing the window. "Tomorrow is another long day. Jumper has to let the family hear the message and then you all have to pack and ship his things back to Montana."

"Yeah, let's get out of here," said Jumper.

The three of them stood up and headed for the door. After all three were out, Katy locked the two locks on the door and then turned and handed Jumper the keys. They all walked down the stairs and out to the street. Jumper hugged Katy, shook hands with Conrad, and hailed a cab. Conrad walked Katy the few blocks to her apartment, gave her a hug and a kiss on the cheek, before she retired to her apartment. He then turned and slowly walked to his own place to get some sleep.

~

The cab pulled to the front of the Marriot and let Jumper out. He walked into the lobby, to the elevator, and finally to his floor. He used his plastic key card to gain entry into the room and quietly made his way to the sofa bed that he was ready to crash on. He peeled off his shirt and kicked off his shoes and then sat on the edge of the bed. One of the bedroom doors in the suite opened and Mr. Barry, wearing pajama bottoms and a T-Shirt, walked out.

"How you doing Jumper."

"I'm okay. Been a rough day, ya know?"

"I know son. I'm glad you made the trip."

"Thank you sir," Jumper said and then cut his breath short as if he wanted to say something else.

"What's on you mind kiddo?" Mr. Barry said, noticing the internal struggle Jumper was having. After a long pause, Jumper lifted his head and looked at Mr. Barry, who was highlighted only by the city lights that were coming in the window.

"Mr. Barry. Cliff called me just before he died. I didn't tell the detective because it was private, but he left a message for us."

Mr. Barry stood still and looked back at Jumper as if to say "Go on" as only a father can do.

Jumper continued, "He left instructions for me which I have followed through with until this point. I need you to hear the message now so that we can finish what he's asked."

"Let me throw on my jeans and we'll go outside." He turned, went back into his room and closed the door.

Jumper put his shoes and shirt back on and waited a moment.

~

The elevator ride down was wordless. Jumper and Mr. Barry walked through the lobby and out into the nightly hum of the Manhattan streets. They walked up the street a short while before stopping underneath the canopy of a closed clothing store that seemed relatively isolated and well lit. They stood there for a few minutes while Jumper explained everything he had done as per Cliff's instructions leading to this point. Mr. Barry listened intently until he finished. When the story concluded, Jumper pulled out his phone, punched some buttons and handed it to Mr. Barry.

He took the phone and held it closely to his ear, turning his back to Jumper and plugging his other ear with his finger. He listened closely, taking in the message. When it was complete, he asked Jumper to play it again for him. He listened to it four times and then he looked at Jumper and said, "So how do we see this video?" Jumper pulled the disc out of his back pocket and handed it to Mr. Barry.

"I have not watched it Mr. Barry. I honestly don't want to watch it, but I got it from Conrad because Cliff asked me too. I played the message for Conrad so he would give it to me. You have to watch it, and then I'd like your help relaying the message to Calvin and Ms. Barry."

"We'll do that tomorrow Jumper, but I need to watch this now. I'm not going to be able to sleep until I see it."

"You can play it in my laptop, but its back in the room."

"That's fine," Mr. Barry said, "I'll watch it in my room."

They both turned and walked back to the hotel.

CHAPTER NINETEEN

Mr. Barry sat on the side of his bed and looked at the computer screen in front of him sitting on his lap. Jumper told him all he needed to do was put the disc in the side and when the screen popped up, just put the arrow on the "play" key and it would begin the video. After several minutes of mental preparation, he picked the disc up off of the bed and slid it into the slot on the side of the computer.

~

Jumper was lying on his bed with his hands folded on his chest, his legs crossed at the ankle and his eyes wide open looking at the flickers of city lights dancing on the ceiling. The room was quiet, eerily quiet in fact. He knew that Mr. Barry was about to watch his son be murdered. He knew why Cliff wanted his father to see it. He knew why he'd been asked to follow through with his final requests. What he didn't know, however, was why in the world this had to happen. A week ago at this moment, he was lying in bed, in his home in California, getting sleep before teaching camp kids basketball skills. Why did something so drastic have to happen to remind him how little life's day-to-day goings on actually meant?

~

The silence was broken. A muffled sob was fighting its way through the walls of Mr. Barry's bedroom. It hurt. Jumper felt like a dagger was sticking in his throat. He couldn't stand the pain. His nose seemed to close, his eyes filled with tears. He lay there, watching the lights, blurry now, on the ceiling. He had never seen or heard Mr. Barry get emotional. The man was a rock. Finally, it was too much. He'd fought with all of his might, but it couldn't be held. He exhaled a massive amount of air, turned on his side, curled into the fetal position, and sobbed into a pillow as quiet as he could.

CHAPTER TWENTY

Calvin opened his bedroom door, which was opposite his fathers, and walked into the main room. The opening door stirred Jumper and he sat up immediately as Calvin walked into the bathroom. Jumper rubbed his puffy sockets while the door to Mr. Barry's room opened. He looked like hell. Huge dark circles surrounded his bloodshot eyes and his nose was fire engine red. He came in and sat on the end of Jumpers sleeper bed.

Calvin exited the bathroom with a face towel drying his freshly washed face. "Mornin' Dad, Jumper."

"Mornin son," Mr. Barry said as he got up and took his turn in the bathroom. Calvin replaced the space that his father had just vacated and looked at the floor. "Today is gonna suck," he gruffed, "I can't wait to get out of this shit-ass city."

Jumper scooted to the end of the bed and sat next to Calvin. "I'm with you. I'm ready to get out of here too."

They sat and stared at the floor for a moment until Mr. Barry came out of the bathroom. Calvin stood up and said, "I'm going to get dressed." And walked back into his bedroom. Mr. Barry went to do the same while Jumper went to shower.

~

Sally and Ms. Barry took their turn to get the morning coffee. They had both been up and showered for over an hour. They knocked on the door to deliver the coffee. Calvin came out of his room to answer the door. Mr. Barry came out of his room with his phone stuck to his ear. The ladies came in as the shower was turning off. Calvin kissed his Mom and wife, and a series of "yes's, uh-huh's, and okay" was coming from Mr. Barry as he stood by the table in the corner of the room jotting down notes on the hotel stationary. Jumper opened the bathroom door with a T-Shirt on and a towel wrapped around his waist.

"Cal, do you mind if I dress in your room?"

"Of course not," replied Calvin as Jumper walked out and grabbed his bag from the side of the bed and then disappeared into Calvin's room. Mr. Barry was wrapping up his phone call with a "see you there" when he turned to his family.

"The Detective just called. We have to meet him at the courthouse at 9:00 to see the judge. He said he pulled some strings and they are going to release the lotto ticket to us this morning. They made official copies and photos that will suffice as evidence during the trial. He said he'll have two officers escort us to the lotto office to claim the ticket."

"I don't want anything to do with that damn ticket," Ms. Barry barked. Jumper was dressed and entering the room as the conversation was underway.

"I know. I don't either, but we can't just throw it away. We'll figure out what to do with it later," Mr. Barry said.

Jumper interjected, "Don't forget Mr. Barry, Cliff left a last will and testament."

"What the hell are you talking about?" quipped Calvin.

"Relax son," said Mr. Barry, "We'll talk about that later. Your brother had some things in place that he only shared with Jumper, which he shared with me last night."

"Why just last night?" Calvin chirped again.

"Because he was doing exactly what your brother asked. We'll tell you about it after we go to the courthouse," Mr. Barry said.

"Whatever. I hate this fuckin' city," Calvin growled as he stomped through the room and slammed his bedroom door behind him. He packed his bag in a huff. It was his last day in New York City.

~

The Courthouse was packed at 9:00 a.m. They followed the directions that Mr. Barry had written down and were soon sitting outside the office of Judge Michael Shapiro. Detective Nelson was only a couple minutes late and greeted everyone with a smile and a handshake. He stepped inside the office door and informed the receptionist that he had arrived. The receptionist relayed the message as Nelson returned to the hallway with the family. A moment later, the receptionist poked her head out of the door and informed them that the Judge could see them now. Jumper, Sally and Calvin stayed on the bench in the hallway while Mr. and Ms. Barry followed the detectives in the office and finally through another door into the Judge's chambers. He gave them a warm welcome and offered them a seat on the opposite side of his desk.

"I'm very sorry about your loss."

"Thank you," Mr. and Ms. Barry said in unison.

"I've read the initial reports and reviewed the evidence already. As soon as I found out that I would be presiding over this case, I wanted to make sure I was as informed as possible. I want you to know that this will no doubt be an easy conviction. I spoke to Detective Nelson this morning and he informed me that you were probably not aware that a 3rd party has been arrested in connection with this case. There was a man in the bar earlier in the evening that allegedly relayed the information to the two men charged with murder. He is charged with conspiracy and I hope to have him sent away for a long time as well."

"Well that's a relief," Ms. Barry tried to say with optimism.

The Judge continued, "It seems pretty simple that the reason behind these events was that Cliff had a winning lottery ticket. I see it only fit that his family gets the ticket so after speaking with Detective Nelson, taking proper documentation for trial purposes, I'm going to release the ticket into your custody. I think the smartest thing to do is to handle that today. It'll take an hour or so to do all of the paperwork and tax documents. The good news is you will not have to pay estate taxes, only income taxes. New York lottery awards the ticket to the bearer, so you'll officially be the winners of this ticket. I will call over to the office and make sure they are waiting for you so it doesn't take up any more of your day than it needs too. Does that sound okay with you?"

"Yes you're honor." Mr. Barry confirmed.

"Good then," Judge Shapiro said. "You'll just need to fill out a couple forms that we've released the ticket to you and then you can be on your way." He pulled out a clipboard and handed it to Mr. Barry.

~

As they left the courthouse, Sally's cell phone was ringing. She picked it up after seeing that it was Katy calling. Sally promised to call back with a plan in a couple minutes.

~

Out front of the Courthouse was a Crown Victoria parked in front of an NYPD squad car. Detective Nelson recommended that Cliff's parents handle the lottery business while the others find something to do for the next hour or two. They agreed and parted ways. Cliff's parents got into the back of the Crown Victoria while Detective Nelson took the drivers seat. He hit a button and the car chirped as he pulled out of his spot with the squad car following tightly behind them; lights on the roof spinning violently.

~

Sally called Katy back and informed her of the morning's events. Calvin and Jumper stood quietly while Sally and Katy made the plan to fill the next two hours. It was a nice day so they decided to head back up to Central Park. That sounded good to the guys so they found a cab and piled in.

~

Detective Nelson came to a stop in front of 15 Beaver Street in the financial district of downtown Manhattan. He got out of the car, as did the officers in the squad car. He stepped back and had a couple words with them before returning and opening the door to let Cliff's parents out of the car. They got out, looked around at the massive buildings of one of the most famous neighborhoods in the world, and then said goodbye to Detective Nelson. He hopped back in his car and sped off as the two officers followed the Barry's to the entrance of the lottery office. They would wait until they had finished and then give them a ride to their next destination.

The lady behind the window had clearly been informed of the arrival of Mr. and Ms. Barry. As soon as they checked in, she disappeared, then re-appeared through a secure door and ushered them to an office where an official lottery clerk was waiting. He informed them that Judge Shapiro had called, etc...

Ms. Barry insisted that Mr. Barry be the sole claimer of the lotto ticket because she was so disgusted with everything that it stood for. Greed had killed her son, and she wasn't budging on the fact that she wanted nothing to do with it.

There was a ton of paperwork. Identification had to be shown again. Tax forms had to be filled out. Federal, State, and Out of State forms all had to be completed. Mr. Barry hated filling out paperwork. He always had. Ms. Barry wouldn't even help him. She just sat there with an attitude as he slowly filled out the information, occasionally asking the clerk what this was or what that meant. Just over an hour and the paperwork was complete. The money was going to be wired to his bank in Missoula, where it would ultimately end up in a trust fund for Calvin and Sally to send their children to college.

~

The two officers were waiting patiently, as instructed, just outside of the doors of the lottery office. When Cliff's parents came out of the building, they asked where they needed to go.

"I need to call and find out," Ms. Barry said to them. So they waited another minute while she called Calvin and found out where they were to meet. "We're going to The Boathouse in Central Park."

The officers walked them to the squad car and put them in the back of the car. Neither of them had ever been in the back of a squad car and both were shocked at how little the space for their legs was. The officers apologized and joked that it's usually a much different character that gets to sit back there. The ride was less than 15 minutes and they arrived at The Boathouse. The officers let them out and jumped back in their car to no doubt do some crime fighting.

Katy was waiting at the entrance. She hugged both of them and then announced, "We're actually over there at the Conservatory Water." She pointed across the road and down a little path from The Boathouse. "People rent little sailboats and drive them around the little pond. We found an empty bench and decided to wait for you there." Katy led the way until they found Jumper, Calvin and Sally sitting quietly.

CHAPTER TWENTY-ONE

Mr. Barry decided to take the lead. It was going to be very hard for Calvin to hear the dying voice of his brother and the message that he'd left for him. Calvin was definitely the most hotheaded one in the family and even his father wasn't sure how he'd react. Ms. Barry had taken a seat on the bench next to Sally and looked off at the sailboats. They needed to go to Cliff's place and pack his things but nobody was in a hurry to do that since it would only lead to more tears.

Mr. Barry walked over to Calvin and put his hand on his shoulder, "C'mon son, lets take a walk."

Ms. Barry quickly asked, "Where are you going?"

"I need to talk to Jumper and Calvin in private. We'll be back in a few minutes."

"I don't like that idea," she refuted, as she was clearly irritated.

"It'll only be a couple minutes," Mr. Barry said as Jumper and Calvin were getting to their feet. Ms. Barry kept her mouth shut and looked back at the water, but her body language was strongly protesting the current plan.

The three men walked north around the perimeter of the reservoir until they found a path and disappeared into the trees. They walked along the path and under a bridge until they found themselves standing next to Cedar Hill. There were a few people scattered about the famous undulating hill, but there was plenty of room for some privacy. They walked up the hill a bit and stopped under a large tree. Calvin turned to Jumper and his father and said, “Alright, what’s going on?”

Mr. Barry looked at his son and said, “Your brother was able to make a phone call before he died. He called Jumper and left us a message.”

Calvin was already fidgeting, “Why would he call Jumper, why wouldn’t he call you or me?”

“I don’t know son, but I can assume it was because he didn’t want to make a choice. Knowing your brother, he wanted to call everybody at the same time and figured that calling Jumper would be the best way to do that.”

“That doesn’t make any sense,” Calvin replied, “but whatever. What did the message say? Since we’re all supposed to ‘hear’ it together.”

Jumper took the cue and pulled his phone out of his pocket. He looked at Calvin and his father and said, “I’ll leave you two alone. I’m gonna go back down by the girls.” He punched some buttons on the phone and handed it to Calvin before turning back down the hill and under the bridge.

Calvin took the phone and looked at it. The screen was waiting for the final command to play the message. He looked at his father, then back at the phone and moved his finger to the button that was waiting to be pressed and play the message. He stuck the phone to his ear, plugged his other ear, looked at the ground and listened. Almost instantly he fell to one knee. Mr. Barry looked off into the distance. If anybody ever claimed that pain was not visual, they were clearly mistaken. He couldn't watch Calvin, he couldn't watch the pain.

Calvin's mouth was open, he couldn't catch his breath, and tears were pouring from his eyes. He was frozen for what seemed like forever, until his body finally seized up and required him to inhale. He let out a wail that turned the heads of anybody within earshot of Mr. Barry and his son. The phone had fallen from his grip and into the grass while Calvin fought for another breath. Once he caught it, he jumped up and took off running at a full sprint up Cedar Hill. He was moving like a runaway train, up the steep hill to the top and beyond. Mr. Barry watched as Calvin disappeared over the hill. He stood there quietly and waited as tears began to fill his eyes.

Calvin didn't know where he was or where he was going. He landed on the East Drive, which travels along the other side of the hill. He headed north, at a full sprint, and didn't quit. He was moving so fast that the tears were actually drying before they hit the bottom of his face. He ran and ran. Full-on sprint until he couldn't go any farther. He'd travelled just over a quarter mile when his body locked up. He was crippled over trying to catch his breath. When he was finally able to move again, he looked up and saw the entrance to the Jacqueline Kennedy Onassis Reservoir. The anger was gone. The crying had stopped. The breathing was still heavy, but he ran the rage out of his system. He turned around and began the fifteen-minute walk back to his father with Cliff's words replaying over and over in his head.

~

Mr. Barry was sitting on the ground with his back leaned up against the tree that they were standing under when Calvin heard the message. Calvin walked down the hill that he'd just sprinted up as his father stood up. They embraced in a big hug but didn't share a word. There was no need. Cliff had said all that needed to be said.

~

When Calvin and his father returned to the conservatory water, it was clear that Ms. Barry was even more irritated than before. She tried to pry information out of Jumper but got nowhere and was getting impatient. She relaxed a little when she turned and saw Calvin and his father walking toward them. Jumper stood up as they got closer and he and Calvin embraced in another silent bear hug.

Mr. Barry stood next to the bench and looked at the sailboats. Calvin turned to his mother and said, "Okay Mom, let's go for a walk."

She stood up without hesitation but was clearly still irritated that she had been put on hold. Calvin and Mr. Barry decided that Calvin should be the one to relay the story and be there when she heard the message. It was not going to be easy, but again, it was Cliff's wishes.

Calvin took his mother's arm and they walked south along the water and around a corner. They walked about 10 minutes as Calvin told the story up to this point, explaining Cliff's last call. She was as irritated as Calvin that the last call was not made to an actual family member, but that was Cliff. He always wanted to be fair to everyone. They found a clearing that had a large rock that seemed like a great place to sit. Calvin pulled Jumper's phone from his pocket and punched the keys to get the voicemail. She took the phone and listened, immediately welling up with tears, which became a full on cry when the message was finished. She set the phone down and buried her face in Calvin's chest. She didn't move for a half hour.

CHAPTER TWENTY-TWO

Mr. Barry, Katy and Jumper had explained everything to Sally when Calvin and his mother returned. Now that everybody was in the know, the mood was much more relaxed. They hatched out a plan for the rest of the day as it was already after 1:00 p.m. They decided to call Conrad and invite him to lunch before heading over to Cliff's apartment. He accepted and the seven of them met at a café close to Cliff's apartment, sat at three two-top tables pushed together in an outdoor garden in the back. The weather was beautiful, the conversation was much easier, and the food was being eaten at full throttle.

After lunch, Conrad assured the family that he'd be in Missoula on Monday and wished them luck for the rest of their stay. Mr. Barry paid the check and they all headed out the front of the café and followed Katy to Cliff's apartment. They walked into the building after Jumper handed the keys back to Katy so she could work the locks. As she opened the door, she couldn't believe how stuffy it was inside. One day with a closed window and the atmosphere was completely different. She immediately walked to the window and opened it.

It was amazing how small the apartment was now with six people standing in the middle of the room. Sally and Katy both went for the Papasan chair, which could easily fit both of their tiny figures. Mr. Barry stood by the window, Jumper sat in the desk chair, and Calvin and his mother sat on the side of the bed.

Jumper took charge. "Okay. We've all heard the message. At the end of it, I was to find a phone book. As you know, last night, Conrad, Katy and I came here to retrieve it. After we found it, we put it back exactly as it was because there was nothing in it for me. I guess he just wanted to make sure that it was found but it didn't really matter who found it, which I didn't know until last night. So here it is."

Jumper leaned down and took the phone book from under the wastebasket. He set it in the middle of the floor, and flipped it open. Everybody just looked at it for a moment. Jumper then leaned over and picked up the envelope on top. He set it aside and pulled out the envelope with the cash and set it next to the other envelope before pulling the DVD out and setting it on the floor as well.

Everybody wanted to reach in and grab and read what was in front of them, but nobody wanted to make the first move. Jumper finally said, "So the DVD has a note inside. It says that nobody is allowed to watch it. He wants it to be played at his funeral."

Ms. Barry could take no more; she reached down and snatched it up. She pulled the note out and gasped at the title that revealed itself under the note.

"If I Die" She set the disc on the bed and read her oldest son's handwriting out loud, "Play this DVD at my funeral. Do NOT watch it beforehand. I appreciate it." She looked at Mr. Barry and snapped, "Well I don't know how we can do that!"

He calmly replied, "We'll figure it out. No need to get into it now."

Jumper continued on, "The sealed envelope says that it is only to be opened by his parents and his brother, and the third envelope is stuffed with cash."

Nobody moved until Calvin finally interrupted the awkwardness, "Well we're all here, why don't we just open it?"

"I'm okay with that if you're father is," Ms. Barry said.

"I don't know. Do you think we should wait and do it with a lawyer? He has it sealed and postmarked so that it is official. It's like the poor man's way of copyrighting."

"Well I don't think anybody in this family is going to argue about who gets what. I assume we'll all respect his wishes and do whatever he wants. There is no reason to pay a stupid lawyer to do exactly what we're going to do anyway."

"I agree with Mom," Calvin added.

"Okay then," Mr. Barry conceded, "Go ahead."

Jumper leaned over and picked up the sealed envelope and handed it to Ms. Barry, who looked at it for a moment and then handed it to Calvin. "You open it," his mother said, "I think I'd like you to read what it says." Calvin looked at his father who nodded with approval. He looked back down at what he was holding, paused a moment, then worked his finger under the corner flap and carefully opened the envelope.

~

"Hello Mom. Hello Dad. Hello Calvin. And Hello Sally, I'm sure you are here as well." Everybody laughed at the first line of the last will and testament. Leave it to Cliff to add comic relief when sending a message from the after life. "If you're reading this, then obviously I'm not with you anymore, so whatever happened, I'm sorry to put you through this. I will only say that I love each of you with all of my soul, and I went to the grave with a full heart." Sally was surprisingly the first to start to cry, but everybody was tearing up within a minute. "So here is my Last Will and Testament. I don't have much so this will be easy. I left $5000.00 that I've saved over the years in an envelope with this letter and a DVD. That money is to cover any expenses that this is costing any of you. Please use it to pay for any funeral costs, including a casket and all the crap." Again with the comic relief as everybody was laughing through their tears. "I hope it's enough and I apologize if it isn't. If there is any left over, donate it to Jake and tell him to get some new equipment for the gym. Please give my snowboard to Jumper, I get sick of watching him rent that junk at the lodges!" Another laugh filled the air and Jumper had tears running down his face. "The only other thing I have that matters is my stock portfolio. I'm writing this on January 1st and it's worth a little over 50k right now. Who knows where it'll be when you read this, but hopefully it's a lot more. The password to my

E*TRADE account is written in a tiny notebook kept underneath the keyboard on my computer. Actually, the passwords to all of my online business is in there, so pull that out when closing my bank accounts and my facebook account and anything else you find in there. I want the stock money to be divided four equal ways. You can liquidate it or just have a brokerage firm divide the shares equally. One share goes to Mom, one to Dad, one to Calvin and Sally, and one to Grandma and Grandpa. Please tell them to take a well-deserved vacation. You guys can do whatever you want with your shares. Everything else is useless. As far as my clothes, computer, all that other stuff, I'm putting Calvin and Sally in charge of distributing or throwing away. None of it is special, so give it to Good Will or whatever. I don't expect that you will, but please do not fight, bicker or argue over anything that belonged to me. None of it matters. Thank you so much! Again, I'm sorry you have to be reading this! I love you!" Calvin folded the paper and put it back in the envelope.

~

The sound of a horn jump-started everybody back into reality. The clock on the nightstand said 3:12. Mr. Barry took charge. He and Calvin were going to take a cab and get a small moving truck from Ryder Truck Rental. Jumper and Katy were to find a UPS store and buy some boxes to pack Cliff's things. Sally and Ms. Barry could begin to pull things out and organize for the pack. It wouldn't take long with all six of them working, but they needed to get moving. Jumper was catching a late flight to California tonight and Calvin and Mr. Barry had a long 36-hour drive ahead of them. Sally and Ms. Barry would catch a flight back tomorrow afternoon.

It was 4:40 pm when Mr. Barry and Calvin returned with the rental truck. They maneuvered into a parking space in front of Cliff's building and buzzed the apartment. When they got inside, most of the work was done. The boxes were packed and the electronics disconnected. Everything was labeled and taped properly. Sally and Katy left to get drinks and sandwiches while the boys began hauling boxes down to the truck. Ms. Barry acted as if she was in charge, recommending this and telling them to do that, but nobody was actually listening to her. It just gave her something to do. After a quick conversation, they decided to leave the bed and computer desk behind, so they put it on the curb with a note that said, "FREE! IN GOOD SHAPE and CLEAN! TAKE IT IF YOU WANT IT." The girls returned with the food and drinks and everybody sat on the floor of Cliff's apartment, tired and sweaty, their minds partially off of their deceased loved one.

~

Mr. Barry and Calvin wanted to shower before starting their two-day trek across the country. They had already checked out of their suite because none of the men were staying at the hotel this evening. They locked the apartment up and congregated on the street in front of the building. Katy had been thinking about something over the last 24 hours and finally decided to muster up some courage and ask, "I was wondering if any of you would mind if I talked to the leasing company about taking over Cliff's lease. I love this apartment and I can afford it at this stage of my life, but I would totally understand if you thought it would be inappropriate."

"Hell no! I don't think that's inappropriate at all," Mr. Barry practically yelled. "Do you?" he asked in the direction of Ms. Barry.

"Not at all sweetheart. I'm sure Cliff would love to have you move into his place. You practically lived together anyways." Ms. Barry said with a touch of orneriness in her voice and a smirk on her face.

"What a relief," Katy said, "For some reason I was afraid it would be wrong to request such a thing, but I decided to ask because I couldn't figure out what that reason was!" Everybody laughed at the silliness of the situation and Katy loosened up again.

"Well do you need this bed or this desk?" Calvin asked.

Katy's face winced a little as she sheepishly replied, "That would be nice."

"Oh for cryin' out loud," Calvin complained sarcastically. "Open those doors up and lets haul this back upstairs."

Jumper and Calvin grabbed the mattress while Mr. Barry grabbed the desk chair and within 10 minutes, the apartment was partially furnished again. They again united on the sidewalk and said their goodbyes. Katy would be in Missoula on Monday, as would Jumper. Hugs were squeezed out and cheeks were kissed before Katy bid adieu to Jumper and the Barry family.

They took two cabs to the hotel. Jumper grabbed his bag and laptop computer from Sally and Ms. Barry's room, apologized for the quick departure, and rushed off to catch a cab and get to the airport. The Barry men each grabbed a fast shower, grabbed their bags and said goodbye to the Barry women. They had a very long drive ahead of them and didn't want to waste any more time. Ms. Barry assured Mr. Barry that she could handle driving the rented SUV back out to the airport and return it safely before their flight tomorrow.

Calvin and his father grabbed a cab back to Cliff's apartment and started fighting traffic on the way out of the city in a moving truck. Calvin voted to drive first, and Mr. Barry was asleep before they even made it across the George Washington Bridge.

Sally and Ms. Barry decided to shower and treat themselves to a nice dinner and a martini or three before the night was over. The concierge recommended a great little place that had wonderful Mediterranean cuisine and two doors away was a lounge with a live piano. It had been the longest week of their lives so a ladies night was easily justified. Besides, that's what Cliff would have wanted.

CHAPTER TWENTY-THREE

It was the first morning all week that the wake-up call was necessary for Sally and Ms. Barry. Both bolted upright immediately on the first ring, looked at each other and began to laugh. The 2nd ring was painful and Sally covered her ears as Ms. Barry reached over and grabbed the phone, stuck it to her ear, said thank you and returned the receiver to its resting place. She flopped back down on her pillow and rubbed her temples. "I should not have had that last cocktail. I haven't felt this fuzzy in years." Sally just giggled and laid her head back down as well.

~

The sun was chasing the Ryder truck from behind as Mr. Barry was now at the wheel. Calvin was sound asleep in the passenger seat. If they could keep up the schedule, alternating sleeping and driving, they would not have to stop outside of food and gas and arrive in Montana Saturday morning. They had just under 24 hours left and were making excellent time.

~

It was a slow start, but Ms. Barry finally made it to the shower. Sally walked down and retrieved Starbucks to continue the tradition and jump-start the day. She returned and showered while Ms. Barry sipped her coffee and got dressed. Sally finished her shower, did the same, and they packed their bags for the flight home. They had to be at the airport three hours early since they had to return their SUV and get their cargo checked in. Ms. Barry never thought she would have to fly across the country with her deceased child locked in the belly of an airplane. Just the idea of it quickly sobered the mood.

After double-checking that they had left nothing, the Barry ladies checked out of the hotel and retrieved their oversized SUV from the valet. Ms. Barry cursed Mr. Barry for being so stubborn about driving themselves in from the airport. It would have been so much easier to simply take a car service. She shook her head at the thought that they were once married, even though it seemed like another lifetime.

Sally navigated while Ms. Barry drove. Picking the correct lanes, reading the signs, and finding exits were a task that Sally had mastered since being married to Calvin. She was better than a GPS system!

After finding JFK airport and then finding the rental return area, writing down the mileage displayed on the odometer, they finally got out of the hulking vehicle and grabbed their bags. They found the counter, handed over the keys, took the receipt and headed into the airport to find the Special Services office.

Sally called Calvin on his cell phone since it was getting to be late morning. She figured he was up and she was correct. He was still riding passenger, but the last stop for gas roused him from his slumber. Sally reported to Ms. Barry that everything was moving as planned, making good time, getting enough sleep, etc...

They found an information desk, which pointed them to the special services unit but they had to check in and go through security before getting there. They went to the kiosks and began the ritual, slipped in their credit cards to check in, their boarding passes were found, they were not checking bags, boarding passes were printed and they were off to security.

The line was moving quickly. They took out their drivers licenses, handed them to the security personnel along with their boarding passes, threw their belongings and shoes into the plastic tubs and walked through the metal detectors. After they put their shoes back on and grabbed their bags, they headed to the Special Services office that they had been directed to.

Ms. Barry stepped to the desk as Sally took a seat across the way from the office. The lady in the office didn't seem to care that Ms. Barry was there transporting a dead body, much less the body of her own son. She felt like she could have been checking in an exotic car and received the same treatment.

After confirming that the coffin had been delivered and was waiting to be loaded into the plane, the Special Services lady took Ms. Barry's credit card and identification while handing her a clipboard with more paperwork to fill out. She hurried through it, handed it over, signed the credit card slip and took her receipt and claiming information that she would need in Missoula. She walked out of the office and checked the time as she walked over to Sally. They had an hour and a half to kill before they had to find their gate and board their flight. Ms. Barry recommended getting a drink and the surprised Sally quickly accepted.

~

Sally called Calvin when they arrived in Missoula. He asked if everything went okay with Cliff, and she told him that his mother was at the counter to claim the cargo now. Calvin was driving now so he wanted to keep the conversation to a minimum. He promised to check in one more time before the sun went down. Sally hung up and waited for Ms. Barry to finish claiming her son.

~

The funeral home had the hearse waiting to pick up Clifford. Ms. Barry finished her paperwork and confirmed that the correct funeral home was indeed picking up the correct coffin, though the likelihood that two bodies would be flying into Missoula on the same day was slim.

Ms. Barry found Sally and they walked to the long-term parking lot. They gave each other a hug, promised to chat in a few hours and got in their respective vehicles to go to their homes. They were exhausted again, and a nap was only minutes away in both houses.

CHAPTER TWENTY-FOUR

The Ryder truck pulled into Calvin's driveway just before 9:00 a.m. Saturday morning. Both Barry men jumped out of the truck and stretched as if they'd just been hatched out of an egg. They walked up to the front door and Sally was opening it. As Mr. Barry walked in, the fragrance of fresh brewed coffee made him perk up. He walked to the kitchen and poured himself a cup with Sally and Calvin right behind him.

They quickly covered the drive. Nobody got pulled over; there were a few thunderstorms, a lot of dead deer on the side of the interstate in

Pennsylvania, and way too many gas station bathroom visits. They finished their coffee and headed for the truck. The plan was simply to put everything in Calvin and Sally's basement until they had the time or inclination to sort through it.

The task was completed in less than 30 minutes. While Sally called Ms. Barry to inform her that the boys were home and safe, Calvin followed his Dad to the Ryder rental place, waited for him to return the rental truck and drove him to the airport so he could retrieve his pickup truck. They planned to speak tomorrow and get ready for the visitation scheduled for Monday.

CHAPTER TWENTY-FIVE

The Missoula Airport was looking to have a busy Monday. By busy, it meant that they were expecting about 100 more arrivals than they usually processed on a Monday. They were coming from all over the country. Friends from college and people that had moved away from Montana that'd he'd worked with or played sports with. For every person that was coming into Missoula, there were three that couldn't make it. The flower shops were working around the clock to fulfill the orders and the funeral home was quickly running out of space if they wanted any room for actual people. The visitation was scheduled for 6:00 to 9:00 p.m.; however, the funeral director asked the family to be there at 5:00 and plan to stay until 11:00, explaining that when somebody this young passes away, the crowd tends to be much bigger than a "normal" visitation and funeral service.

~

More than half of the passengers on the Delta flight that was expected to land at 1:20 p.m. in Missoula were on the plane to attend services for Cliff. It was an inbound flight from Minneapolis where the flights from Newark, Austin, and Boston had dropped everyone for their layovers. Conrad, Katy, Pedro and Reina were passengers, as were several of the customers that had frequented The Tan Hat Man over the last several years. The ride was festive, the passengers were drinking as if they were in the bar and the chatter level was at a much higher decibel than that of a normal flight. It was exactly what Conrad expected, but Pedro was feeling a little guilty that everyone seemed so happy. He almost forgot that this was a bar crowd; blue collar, white collar, every age, sex and race, always looking for a reason go party. Cliff would have loved it.

When the plane landed, there was a Holiday Inn Shuttle waiting just outside of baggage claim. Most of the people coming in had booked their hotel on a discount website and the 3-star hotel that was the cheapest on all of the sites was the Holiday Inn. When everyone on the plane realized that they were all going to be staying at the same place as well, the festivities found another gear. They piled into the shuttle bus and it pulled out of the airport. When they arrived, they grabbed their baggage, tipped the driver, and waited in line at check in. Some decided to catch a nap before heading to the wake, while others decided to meet in the bar that resided in the hotel. Pedro and his wife had a room two doors down from Katy, and Conrad was just one floor above. They decided to meet in the lobby at 5:00. Conrad had already set up a ride for the four of them to get to the funeral home.

~

Calvin and Mr. Barry were not looking forward to this night in any way. Shaking hands with several hundred people and hearing what a great guy Cliff had been seemed more like intentional torture than loving comfort. They were not looking forward to more tears, especially the fake ones from the overly dramatic types that had a story to tell about a time Cliff had affected them, the operative word being "a;" one single boring story or moment when Cliff made them laugh or helped them out and apparently changed their lives forever. Every wake has them, and they always suck, but as the family, you just grin and bear it.

~

The casket was closed. Inside, the battered body of Cliff lay peacefully but nobody was going to see it. There were no repairs that could ready his face for a viewing of the general public. His parents also wanted the memory of Cliff to be that of his engaging smile and warm demeanor, not stitched up, bruised version of the young man they all knew. The entire Barry family was there by 4:30, as was Jumper. They congregated in the main room and read through the many cards attached to the endless bouquets of flowers sent from family, friends and other acquaintances. More than half of the flowers had been sent from faceless names residing in New York, no doubt people that had spent some sort of significant amount of time with him. A few were addressed to the Barry Family & Katy. It was beautiful.

Next to the head of the casket was an easel with a very large picture of Cliff resting securely on it. It had flowers nicely placed on the top two corners and slightly hung down, framing the photo. It was a picture taken at Christmas from two years ago where he was in a very nice sweater with a collared shirt underneath it, poking up around his neck. There was obviously a Christmas tree in the background, but it had been cropped and blown up to primarily feature Cliff's gorgeous young face and model worthy smile.

At the foot of the casket on the right side, was another easel holding a collage of photos. There were close to 100 pictures all surrounding an 8x10 of Cliff with his brother. They detailed his entire life. There were a couple of baby pictures and toddler pictures including the standard bubble bath where he and Calvin had bubbles everywhere. There was a picture of Cliff shuffling around in his father's shoes that were massively oversized. There were some grade school photos, some photos of different Halloween costumes and playing in piles of raked up leaves, a little league baseball "card" with his stats printed on the bottom. There were pictures of him playing high school football and pictures of him in Jake's sparring with his brother. His grandparents smiled proudly in some photos with their grandchildren. Jumper made the board a few times with snaps of them shooting hoops in the college gym, snowboarding, and digging into a Thanksgiving dinner. Two carefully selected photos of he with his mother and he with his father were on the center of the board, one on each side of the center picture of he and Calvin. There was also a very fun snapshot of Katy and Cliff in Central Park that somebody had snapped when she had jumped on his back and was biting his ear. It was a lovely memorial, and many pictures were taken of the pictures throughout the evening.

Under the easel were a couple of personal belongings that defined him. His helmet from his high school football team, a pair of very used boxing gloves, a hunting knife, an old lift ticket from a weekend on the slopes, a book on investing, a bottle opener, a very tattered stuffed animal that he'd clearly had since he was a baby, and a copy of Pete's Dragon on DVD. It was impossible to completely define him, but they did the best they could.

~

The funeral director was correct, and people did indeed show up early. The first arrived at 5:20 and stood outside of the entrance until the door was officially open. It was an assistant coach from his high school football team that was also a fireman. He snuck away from the firehouse and hoped to beat the crowd and pay his condolences and return to work. Mr. Barry recognized him and stepped outside to chat.

Other cars, trucks and SUVs began to enter the lot and park on the street and empty out. Everybody was well dressed and quiet, and they began to form a line at the door. Mr. Barry went back inside and checked on everybody, made sure everyone was ready, and asked the funeral director if they could indeed open the doors early. At 5:35, the funeral director opened the door and people started to file in, slowly of course, because each paused to sign the guest book before entering.

There were 70 chairs arranged nicely in seven rows of ten each, split in half with an isle down the middle. After signing in, people would take a right and enter the room with Cliff at the far end, walk by the chairs, stop and look at the collage, walk past the casket, say a prayer or touch it or whatever ritual made them feel better, stop again and look at the lovely poster size picture at the head of the casket, then begin the greetings, handshakes and hugs. Ms. Barry was first with Calvin immediately after and finally Mr. Barry. Cliff's grandparents were sitting with Sally in the first five chairs almost next to Mr. Barry.

The fireman was the first to come through. He hugged Ms. Barry and visited with Calvin for a bit, having coached him as well. He'd already caught up with Mr. Barry so another handshake and a pat on the shoulder was enough. He turned around, shook the hands of Cliff's grandparents and Sally, and made his way out of the funeral home. Mr. Barry's best friend and co-worker for most of his career, Tim Sweed and his two sons, had arrived early and sat close to the front for a couple hours after making their way through the line. Katy, Conrad, Pedro and Reina were near the front of the line as well and went through the same ritual; taking a seat about halfway back in the rows of chairs. Jumper was up and down, tending to the needs of all of them, getting water and tissues or helping the elderly move through the compact space. And so it went for the next five hours.

People who had never met his parents or brother introduced themselves and explained their relationship with the deceased. Friends from grade school, old teachers and coaches, teammates, co-workers, high school classmates, college friends, friends of the family that didn't know Cliff personally, and even his childhood dentist. People took their time remembering, looking at the photos, saying their prayers and visiting with the family. Some handed the family a keepsake of some sort; a photo they shared with Cliff or a religious keepsake dear to them, and even a song on a disc that somebody so moved had wrote and recorded since hearing the news. Those from New York seemed to congregate around Conrad and crew after respects had been made, but nobody overstayed their welcome, though some probably had one too many cocktails before arriving.

At 10:40 p.m. the funeral director closed the door and the family sat and softly chatted for a bit. They were all on their way home by 11:00 as the funeral service was to start at 10:00 a.m. tomorrow and would no doubt be more emotional than the visitation had been.

~

Back at the bar at the Holiday Inn, the bar was busy with more than twenty New Yorkers including Katy, Conrad, and Pedro and Reina. Katy and Reina weren't drinking alcohol, but Conrad and Pedro were knocking them back with the rest of them. There were at least fifty toasts to Cliff before they were forced to retire to their rooms by 1:00 a.m.

CHAPTER TWENTY-SIX

Most of the flowers that were on display at the visitation had been moved to make room for chairs for people attending the funeral service. Some went home with the family, some were taken to the cemetery, and the others were put in the basement of the funeral home to be collected later.

There were 160 chairs in the funeral parlor now. Calvin was worried that it was too many and mentioned that he would be upset if they over estimated and the room wasn't full. The funeral director promised him that they would still be short on seats, he'd done this many times and he knew the numbers.

Jumper and the entire Barry family were there by 9:00 Tuesday morning. Calvin declined the request to give the eulogy on Sunday so they asked if Jumper could do it. He'd be honored. They visited with the pastor for a bit, discussed the order of things and what would be said and stirred about the room in discomfort as the finality of the whole process was coming to a close. They took the entire front row of seats for themselves and made sure that Jumper, Katy, Conrad, Pedro and Reina were considered part of the family today by saving seats for them as well.

The doors were open at 9:30 and people began to file in. It was quiet, a small hum of conversation filling the air as people took a place in a chair. A cell phone erupted and dirty looks were fired from all over the room, making everybody double check to be sure that their phones were silenced as well. By 9:55 the funeral director was proven correct, and there were no more seats. The latecomers filed in around the back and on the sides, as it was now a standing-room-only affair.

At precisely 10:00, the pastor took his place before the podium that now resided a couple of feet in front of the coffin, Cliff's poster sized photo on the easel still resided at the head of the coffin, but the easel at the foot had been replaced by a very large flat screen TV on a stand that overlooked the room. The room was instantly hushed as the pastor began. He started with a prayer and then a personal story of an encounter he shared with Cliff, another prayer and some fond memories the family had shared with him. He then introduced Jumper as Cliff's best friend and friend to the family, and invited him up to give the eulogy.

~

Jumper stood from his seat in the front and shook hands with the pastor before stepping up to the podium. The pastor stepped to Jumper's left and stood on the other side of the TV. Jumper looked out at the crowd and cleared his throat.

"Ladies and gentleman, the Barry family and I would like to thank you for being here this morning. This is a sad day, one where we have lost something dear to us, and that is the life of Clifford James Barry. I could talk about Cliff for hours, telling you endless stories of the amazing friend and person that he was, but most of you know that. I'm only going to tell you one story, one that his family and I discussed in great detail because it is very personal and very private, but we came to the conclusion that the story encompassed the man the Cliff was. It defined how selfless and thoughtful he was. It is the story of the last thing he did before he died." The crowd was motionless, listening with great intent as Jumper began the story. "Most of you know that Cliff was mercilessly killed in a bar fight where he worked in New York City. I've been told it was just before closing when two strangers came in to rob him. We can only assume that Cliff fought back because he feared for his life. Cliff was a very smart guy. So after the fight, after the assailants had left the bar and Cliff lay on the floor, battered and broken, he was able to fish his cell phone out and make one last phone call." Jumper choked up for a minute, dropped his chin and took a half step back, composed himself and stepped back to the podium. "He called me as I slept in my bed in San Diego, completely unaware that my best friend was dying. He left a message for me, but the message was for me to relay several other messages." Jumper again choked up but didn't move this time. He held his ground at the podium with fierce determination to get through the remainder of his speech. "So I give you Cliff Barry's last words. His message said," tears were streaming down his face, his voice was cracking, but he growled his throat clear and continued, "Hey brother, I love you man. This is it for me. You have to do me a favor. Tell my Mom it doesn't hurt. Tell my Calvin he has to let it go, no revenge. Make sure my Dad sees the security tapes so he knows I never quit, and tell Katy I love her. Last thing, there is a DVD in my apartment titled..."

And that was the cue for the pastor to turn on the DVD player. Jumper stepped away from the podium and sat down in his seat. The lights were dimmed.

CHAPTER TWENTY-SEVEN

The screen was black then faded to white. Big blue letters appeared. Small gasps and sniffles were heard around the room. Tears were instantly flowing. Tissues and handkerchiefs were being yanked out of every pocket and purse. The screen said:

Thank You!

For 27 Years of Life and Love!

The lettering vanished and the picture faded into Cliff, sitting Indian style in his papasan chair in a pair of sweatpants and a T-Shirt with a bandana tied snuggly around his head. He had a bottle of Gatorade resting in the middle of his lap. He was smiling and looking straight into the camera lens. He looked calm, peaceful, and happy. After a moment, he spoke.

"Hello everyone! I am really glad you are here. You can't possibly know how much it means to me. Unfortunately, the circumstances that called you here couldn't possibly be something you're happy about. But let me assure you, this is a celebration; a time to be excited, to reflect, and to understand the things that are important to you. I'm not gonna sit here and preach to you or try to guess how you could be feeling. What I'm simply doing is telling you a few stories, a few thoughts and ideas, and a few reasons why we are going to celebrate today. I'm going to explain to you what I've learned in my young 27 years of life, and hope that you can take something away from it."

Cliff took a swig from his Gatorade bottle and shifted his seat in the chair before replacing the lid and looking back in the camera. Everyone's eyes were fixated on the screen.

"Today is New Years Day. Every year since I was fourteen years old, I've made a video on a VHS tape, and now a DVD. I've never told anyone about it. The title written on the disc is 'If I Die' and I always have left it where I know my brother or parents would find it in the event of my passing. Inside the box with the tape was a note specifically instructing whoever found it that this tape was not to be watched prior to the funeral, and that I would like it played as part of the service. So you should all be watching this for the first time, as I know my family would respect my wishes. That is the story of how this came to be. Oh, and by the way, don't bother trying to find the tapes from previous years; I destroy them after the new one has been recorded." He winked at the camera and flashed his charming smile.

"So where to begin? Let me first explain to you why I've done these tapes every year for all these years. See, I think everybody has something to share with the world, and I don't know if very many people actually ever have a chance to do it. I feel like people often die without tying up loose ends, without saying what they wanted to say, or telling those close to them what they've wanted to tell them but never had the nerve. To let you know, if you are watching this video right now, it is because we had some sort of connection. Maybe you're here as support for one of my parents, or as a friend from college, or an old co-worker or classmate. Even if we've never actually met, you're here for a reason, and that reason is important to me. You've affected me in many ways, most of you directly, some of you indirectly, some of you never even realizing what you've done for me. I want to give an example. Mr. Sweed?" He looked back and forth on the camera as if he could see the crowd. "How you doing sir? I'm sure you're here somewhere because you worked with my father throughout my entire childhood. You are one of his best friends, if not his best friend. Many times at the dinner table or on the weekends, Dad would tell a story from the week or day at work, and you were part of it more times than not, often providing the comic relief from our busy schedules. I only met you once or twice, and it was always brief because it was usually after a game that I'd played in high school, but you are a big part of my fathers' life, and in turn, made a big impact on my life. I remember the stories when I was in grade school and your boys were in high school playing football. Dad would show us the newspaper articles and tell the stories that made those things possible, the stories the public and the papers didn't know. I wanted to be like your boys. I wanted to be in the papers and make my Dad proud. I wanted him to be able to show his friends and co-workers what his boy was capable of doing. When I reached high school, I did just that, and I owe some of that to you. Some of my motivation and work ethic came from the excitement I saw in my Dad because he knew the father of the kid in the paper. You were a mentor to my father because you'd been down the road my father was travelling as a parent just ten or so years prior and I thank you." Cliff shifted his seat, seemed to take a moment for his next thought, and then addressed the camera again.

"That was just one example of how you can affect somebody without even knowing that you're doing it. There are many more in this room right now, and I thank each and every one of you. So what is the point of what I'm trying to say? Well, let me start by giving some thought to the eternal questions we often ask. Again, these are my thoughts at the end of 27 years of life, and every year I looked forward to having different thoughts in the coming years, letting ideas evolve and develop and change. I don't pretend to know anything, in fact, I'm totally aware that I know nothing!" The room loosened up and a chuckle or a laugh was audible throughout. "But I know what I know at 27 years of age, and I feel like its worth expressing, if not to make you reflect, but to make sure you understand that I'm okay with this death thing, and I want you to be okay with it as well. So what is the meaning of all of this? Of life? I don't know. Do you? Does anybody? We all have theories, and mine are pretty simple really. I think the meaning of life is to simply to love and give. Many people along the way have tried to give too much and end up losing the people they were giving to. That's because they were giving them things. Fancy dinners, nice clothes, trips around the world, new cars, and anything else that money can buy is their idea of giving. I feel like I'm lucky enough to have plenty of friends and lots of family, in fact I'm proud of it. My Dad always told me that you're judged by the company you keep. My family never had much to offer but we've always offered ourselves. Our door is always open. We always had enough to offer a sandwich or find the time to play a board game. The number of times that our phone rang in the middle of the night is uncountable. My mom would take the call and stay up all night lending an ear to a friend in need, or Dad would strap on his boots and head out to a farm where a friend had a horse astray because the fence had broken. We gave ourselves, and I took that with me. The point is, whenever I've felt that I was being inconvenienced by someone, I remembered my folks. It is never an inconvenience to give some of you. What else are we here for? Not to take, I'm pretty sure of that.

So this brings me to another thought. Why doesn't anybody say what they mean anymore? Look, if you love somebody, you better tell them. I don't mean in the sense that you just met Mister or Misses Right and you're courting and trying to figure out when to take the relationship to the next level..." His eyes bugged a little and there was a chuckle in his voice. "But I mean on a daily basis. Your friends, parents, husbands, wives, grandparents. Anyone that you enjoy being around. If you need to say I love you, say it! If you've enjoyed their company, say it! If you haven't seen them in ages and you're glad you ran into them, say it! Think about how good you feel when someone is glad to see you or wants to hang out again. If you feel that way, allow them that feeling. The power is yours to give. In keeping with this thought, I'd like to tell you again, I'm really glad you're all here." He smiled and gulped down some more Gatorade, shifted his weight and came back to the room.

"So I feel like I'm getting a little preachy, and I assured you I wouldn't, and I don't want to bore you any longer. I have just one more major point I want to touch on. Many of you here are god fearing Christians, and why wouldn't you be? This is Montana for crying out loud! Since I've moved to New York, however, I've met people from every other belief system probably known to man. There is an amazing thing that has come from that experience, and that thing is: It doesn't matter. If you're a good person, you're a good person. That's it. If you're selfless and giving, then who gives a rats ass what you believe happens when you die. Not a single person in this room knows what happens. In fact, since you're watching this, I'm the only one here that does know!" He laughed at his own joke and again the attendees chuckled. "And I hope I'm standing in the corner over there," he pointed to the left as if looking off the screen to the corner of the room, "smiling at how many of you guys have shown up and how much I love you." There was a pause. Cliff's face went a bit pale for a moment and it was clear is he was choking back a frog in his throat. He cleared his throat, took a drink, and looked back into the crowd through his camera lens.

"The reason I bring this up is because I want you to understand something. I want you to understand why I'm so cool with this death thing and why I'm not afraid. I want you to understand what my idea of heaven and hell is. See, I don't believe that heaven or hell is a place we go when we die. I believe that heaven and hell is the last thing you experience before you die. If you die with regrets, sorrows, mistakes that you haven't tried to reconcile, or people that you didn't do right by, well, then, that my friends, to me, is hell. It is the last thing you'll think about before it all shuts down. Adversely the opposite is heaven! We all make mistakes. We've all hurt someone at some point, but if we do everything in our power to resolve those moments, and if we try our best to do the right thing every chance we get, and if we are humble enough to realize nobody is perfect, and if everybody we love, knows that we love them, then I can't help but to believe that the last thoughts we'd have are that of peace and serenity. So if you're here today, you already know I love you. More importantly, you knew I loved before I died. I truly believe that; everybody I love knows I love them. And that to me is heaven. No matter what the circumstances were that caused this funeral, I ask you not to worry, but to celebrate, because I got to experience heaven."

The screen faded back to white and the blue words came into focus:

I HOPE YOU KNOW

CHAPTER TWENTY-EIGHT

The lights came up and the pastor stepped back to the podium. He closed with an emotional prayer as the room was completely flooded with tears. The service ended and everybody filed out to get into their cars and proceed to the cemetery.

The processional was over five miles long. It took almost an hour before everybody had arrived, parked and made their way to the Missoula City Cemetery for the final words and official burial of Clifford James Barry.

The pastor said a few more words and another prayer was delivered before Cliff was lowered in the ground. Everybody was invited to join the family at their favorite pizza joint downtown and the funeral came to a close.

~

Most of the immediate friends and family stopped in the pizza joint. Jumper was hugged and congratulated time and again for being able to fight through his eulogy, but it was clear he didn't take pride in it. In fact, he was ready to go home to California. Calvin was quiet most of the time as he sat next to his wife. People were delighted to meet Katy. Conrad, Pedro and Reina were made to feel welcome by everyone. Mr. Barry was tired of shaking hands and finally sat down to a frosty mug of beer. Ms. Barry was ready to go home and have one last massive cry.

~

The New Yorkers had again congregated at the bar in the Holiday Inn. Almost all of them were catching the 9:30 p.m. flight back to the east coast and thus had checked out of their rooms. The day had come to an end.

~

Calvin checked the New York papers online everyday for news and updates on the progress of the trial, but as time passed, the articles got smaller and were harder to find. Sally kept in touch with Katy and kept abreast with any news that Calvin couldn't find in the online papers. Conrad was at the entire trial and called Mr. Barry anytime something of importance was delivered. Finally, after eight months, the news came in. Jimmy received life in prison. Rodney was sentenced to 22 years and Pauly earned 15 years.

None of it seemed like enough to Calvin but he remembered Cliff's words on a daily basis. He had to let it go.

Made in the USA
Lexington, KY
21 September 2018